"I've loved you in the dark before . . ."

Neil's lips were at her ear. "Remember, Lacey? Remember what we used to do to each other in bed? You knew how to drive me wild. I want you to do that again, and I'll . . . ."

The rest was breathed hotly into her ear, as Lacey moved her head from side to side, trying not to hear his erotic promises. He knew exactly where to press, where to stroke.

Desperate to resist the effect he was having on her love-starved senses, she finally gasped, "Neil, don't do this. It's too late to start over."

Dear Reader,

We at Harlequin are extremely proud to introduce our new series, **HARLEQUIN TEMPTATION**. Romance publishing today is exciting, expanding and innovative. We have responded to the ever-changing demands of you, the reader, by creating this new, more sensuous series. Between the covers of each **HARLEQUIN TEMPTATION** you will find an irresistible story to stimulate your imagination and warm your heart.

Styles in romance change, and these highly sensuous stories may not be to every reader's taste. But Harlequin continues its commitment to satisfy all your romance-reading needs with books of the highest quality. Our sincerest wish is that **HARLEQUIN TEMPTATION** will bring you many hours of pleasurable reading.

THE EDITORS

U.S.
HARLEQUIN TEMPTATION
2504 WEST SOUTHERN AVE.
TEMPE, ARIZONA
85282

CAN.
HARLEQUIN TEMPTATION
P.O. BOX 2800
POSTAL STATION "A"
WILLOWDALE, ONTARIO
M2N 5T5

For Now, For Always

LYNN TURNER

Harlequin Books

TORONTO • NEW YORK • LONDON
AMSTERDAM • PARIS • SYDNEY • HAMBURG
STOCKHOLM • ATHENS • TOKYO • MILAN

Published April 1984

ISBN 0-373-25108-4

Printed in Canada

1

SOMETHING TOLD Lacey Hartmann to put down the insurance-premium schedule and glance at the slim gold watch on her wrist.

"Damn!" she muttered. Lacey quickly came out from behind her desk, collecting her purse as she headed for the door. "I almost forgot the boys' soccer practice," she explained to the two women in the outer office as she hurried through.

Ellen, the elder of the two, assured her they'd hold the fort until she got back. Lacey flashed a quick smile of gratitude and swept out the door, under the large swinging sign that identified the renovated clapboard house as Meinert Realty & Insurance.

Ten minutes later her silver Audi pulled into the drive of a tri-level redwood-and-stone house on a quiet residential street. Before the car had rolled to a complete stop, two children burst out the front door.

"Gosh, mom, we're gonna be late again." That was seven-year-old Todd, admonishing her as he crawled into the back seat.

"So what—it's no big deal if we're five minutes late." His twin, Scott, the peacemaker, threw Lacey a forgiving grin as he climbed into the front beside her and closed the door. Lacey reached over to ruffle his dark hair before shifting into reverse to back out of the drive.

"Well, almost everybody else is always on time," came the mild grumble from the back seat.

"Almost everybody else has moms who don't do anything but stay home and watch TV all day, too," Scott pointed out reasonably.

"Yeah, but our mom's a *businesswoman*." The smug pride in Todd's voice made Lacey chuckle.

"Well, this *businesswoman* has to to get back to work as soon as I drop you guys off at practice. I hope you had a snack to hold you over until supper. It may be late tonight."

Scott nodded for both of them. "Mrs. Moore made us baloney and cheese sandwiches."

"With ketchup and mayonnaise," Todd put in.

"And dill pickles."

"And chocolate ice-cream cones for dessert."

"Yech!" Lacey commented with an exaggerated shudder, and they all laughed together.

When they reached the soccer-practice pitch she got out to ask Paul Rossi what time she should return to collect the boys. He was showing off for the kids again, she noticed—juggling the soccer ball with feet, knees and muscular thighs, bouncing it off his forehead, ducking under it to catch it with a heel and send it back over his head. Paul loved an appreciative audience, especially if that audience included an attractive woman. When he decided the performance had gone on long enough, he deftly caught the ball in one hand and turned to her with a boyish grin. Lacey smiled back and gave him what he wanted.

"Very impressive. Did you learn all that in Italy or Argentina?"

He shrugged as he walked over to her. Paul had the gait of a natural athlete. He moved lightly, on the balls of his feet, and in the soccer shoes he was wearing now his walk was slightly pigeon-toed. He was altogether a fine specimen, and if she'd been in the market for the kind of casual affair he was geared to, she knew she could have had him at a crook of her little finger. It wasn't a vain thought, merely realistic and a bit regretful.

He stopped a scant foot in front of her. In her three-inch heels Lacey could look him squarely in the eye, and she did, still smiling. Yes, he was certainly a good-looking man: close-cropped dark curly hair, laughing brown eyes and a classic Roman nose above a full, sensual mouth and firm chin.

Paul was thirty, two years older than her, and still a bachelor. He'd come here as consulting engineer for a plastics company from his native Italy, via Argentina, where he'd spent two years doing similar work. Paul was open and warm, with an artless charm that made him easy to talk to and increased his appeal to the opposite sex. His compact body was lean and tough, and the undeniably male aura he projected was all the more potent for being unstudied, completely natural.

Lacey instinctively knew that in bed he would be playful and tender, a considerate, unselfish lover who gave as much as he took. For a moment she was tempted to consider the subtle and sometimes not-so-subtle invitations he'd been sending out for the past year. But only for a moment.

"Both," he said, in answer to the question she'd forgotten asking. "I have played since I was a child, and the company I worked for in Argentina sponsored a team that was very good. Playing there helped to sharpen my skills."

His accent was one of the most attractive things about him, a fact he was well aware of. Lacey had noticed that it became more pronounced when he spoke to a pretty young girl, and it was sometimes even comically exaggerated when there was a really stunning mature woman around. Ironically, though he'd pursued her with more determination than he had any other female in town, the accent all but disappeared when he spoke to her. It was a sign of his respect for her intelligence, she knew. The respect was mutual. With one notable exception, Paul had the finest mind of any man she'd ever known, though he often masked it behind his easygoing charm.

Now he tilted his head to give her a frankly admiring look that ranged from her short, sun-streaked hair, over her tailored ivory linen suit and open-necked blouse of forest green silk, down the shapely curve of her calves to the thin straps of her tan leather sandals.

"You are not staying to watch today?" he asked in disappointment.

Lacey shook her head. "'Fraid not. My In tray overfloweth. When should I come back for the boys?"

"We will be finished by five-thirty, I think. If it's earlier than that, I'll bring them to your office."

"That would be very nice of you, Paul," she said sincerely, and he flashed her a devilish grin.

"Perhaps if I am nice enough to *you*, *cara* . . . ."

The murmured suggestion never got finished, because at that moment one of Lacey's sons darted between them in hot pursuit of a soccer ball.

"Looks like practice has started without you, coach," she chuckled as Paul reached down to catch her offending offspring by an arm.

"If only they would run like that during a match," he muttered wryly, then turned the boy around to see the lettering on the back of his yellow T-shirt. "Well, Scott, since you're so full of energy, you can be spiker today."

The boy looked up with a mischievous grin, and Lacey burst out laughing. At Paul's puzzled expression, she explained.

"They've switched shirts on you again. That's Todd."

Paul shook his head as the boy ran off giggling. "Living with them must be constant confusion, Lacey. How on earth do you tell them apart?"

"They're mine," she answered simply, then gave him a direct, slightly provocative look. "And I can always recognize what's mine, as well as what's not."

"Always?" Paul asked softly.

"Always! I really do have to run, Paul. See you later," she threw over her shoulder as she turned for the car.

It was true that the twins were identical to everyone but Lacey and Mrs. Moore, the widowed neighbor who stayed with them during the day. Even their teachers couldn't tell which was which. But from their birth each had possessed his own distinct personality. Lacey often thought they were like a coin: sometimes back to back, representing the opposite sides; other times so attuned to each other they were like a single entity, the halves merging into a whole.

Physically they were so alike that even their own pediatrician sometimes confused them: soft, thick hair so dark it looked black in certain lights; eyes large and round, of an unusual deep copper color; still small for their ages, as twins often are. Yet despite their slight stature, they were mentally and emotionally mature beyond their years, excelling at whatever athletic activity they threw themselves into. Both swam on the country-club team—at seven, the two youngest swimmers competing in area meets—and now they were showing a natural affinity for soccer, as well.

Paul had shaken his head in perplexity when he praised their talent to her. It went beyond athletic ability, he said, it was almost as if they could read each other's minds. One always knew exactly where the other would be before he got there, what play he would make before he made it. Lacey merely smiled. It was nothing new to her.

Paul was genuinely fond of the boys, she knew. Yet he never tried to exploit his growing friendship with them to get closer to her, a testimonial to his personal code of ethics. As she pulled into her parking space she frowned, remembering something he'd said when the three of them had returned from a week's vacation in Florida the week before. Commenting on how deeply tanned the boys had become, he teased that they must have a drop or two of Italian blood from their father's side of the family.

She had smiled and said no, not that she knew of, but she was secretly upset by the reminder of their father.

He had been thirty-five when she met him, head of his own pharmaceuticals company, self-assured to the point of arrogance. An uncompromising businessman with a deserved reputation for ruthlessness, he had never revealed any details of his past. Others had told her of his difficult childhood as an orphan, shunted from one foster home to another.

Until Paul's casual remark, she hadn't thought of him in months. Oh, it still hurt sometimes to look at the twins; they were so like him, duplicates in miniature of the hard, taciturn man who had fathered them without even knowing it. But most of the time her life was too full for thoughts of the past, and that was the way she wanted it. She'd built a new life for herself, on her own. She was justifiably proud of what she'd accomplished by sheer hard work and force of will, because not many women could have done as much with as little. Not many men, either, in fact.

Until she had married Neil Hartmann, her life had been an easy one. As an only child, she had been denied little. So when attractive, sophisticated Neil proposed to her after a brief courtship, she was dismayed by her parents' response.

Her father pointed out that Neil was too old for her, that their backgrounds were vastly different, that as his wife she would be exposed to a world she'd never known before—expected to entertain his business associates, assist him whenever possible in his dealings with strange people, spend hours and sometimes days alone while he was occupied with company matters and then make herself available as a sounding board when he did come home. But, to a starry-eyed eighteen-year-old, the "arguments" had been all the encouragement Lacey needed to cement her decision.

For the first few weeks their life together had seemed like heaven, but it didn't take long for the stardust to begin to wear off. Neil was practically never at home, and when he was he refused to talk to her about his work or anything else. He treated her like a child—worse, like a doll, to be dressed up and occasionally put on display for his friends and associates. He took pride in her beauty but didn't seem concerned about her mind or feelings. And he was almost obsessively possessive, withdrawing into a grim silence if she made even casual conversation with another man on the rare occasions when they went out.

Lacey had begun to feel she was slowly starving to death for the love he denied her. She tried everything to make him aware of her as his equal, his partner. Nothing worked. Gradually she began to withdraw from him, her pride and her heart shattered by his continued coldness. Eventually the only thing they shared was sex; she couldn't think of it as making love. Not that it wasn't good. Neil was a magnificent lover, but that was only to be expected, she supposed, considering his age and experience.

For almost two years they existed like strangers living under the same roof, communicating only in the darkness of their bedroom, when he would turn to her and drive her out of her mind with pleasure, never speaking, never murmuring soft love words in her ear; telling her with his hands and mouth and body exactly what he wanted from her, and what he was prepared to give in return.

And then, one horrible pain-filled night nearly eight years ago, he had savagely and brutally destroyed whatever feeling she had left for him and ripped her secure world apart at the seams.

ELLEN AND VI were laughing when Lacey entered the office, still under the brooding spell of her lapse into the past. She asked what was funny, and Vi explained.

"It's old man Sawyer. He called while you were out. Now he wants to insure his new *bird dog* against sterility!"

Lacey rolled her eyes, and then joined into their laughter. Royal Sawyer had read about such coverage a year ago in one of his farm journals. Since then he'd bought sterility insurance on a stud bull and a prize Appaloosa stallion.

"Next he'll want us to write a policy on his rooster," Ellen remarked with a grin.

"As long as Mrs. Sawyer doesn't ask for one on *him*," Lacey responded dryly as she headed for her private office.

"At his age!" Vi scoffed. "But can we do it? Insure the bird dog, I mean?"

Lacey left the door open as she went to her desk. "I don't see why not. I'll check for a precedent, but if we can write a policy for a bull or a horse, why not a dog?"

"Oh, I almost forgot!" Ellen followed her, a sheet of notepaper in her hand. "Believe it or not, we got a call about the Miller place."

Lacey sat back in surprise. "You're kidding! Nobody local, I'll bet."

Ellen's expression was wry. "Well, no, but he seemed familiar with the property. Asked if it was the old Miller farm out on Claypool Road. He wanted to see it, but I explained that both our salespeople were out of the office. He said he might just drive out on his own and have a look at the place."

"Let's hope he waits until after dark," Lacey muttered as she held out a hand for the paper.

"Oh, don't be such a pessimist. He could be one of those handyman types looking for a fixer-upper. He sure sounded like a take-charge guy on the phone." Ellen handed over the paper with the potential buyer's name and turned for the outer office. At the door she paused briefly with an encouraging smile. "Besides, I think it's a good omen that he's got the same last name as you. I'll bet we finally unload that place!"

Lacey didn't hear the hopeful prediction. Her eyes were fastened in sick horror on the name Ellen had copied in her elegant script: *Neil Hartmann*.

Her hand shook as she gripped the paper. It couldn't be! Not after all this time!

In the beginning she'd been terrified that her husband might come after her, try to find her. She had used her mother's maiden name for a while, just in case he did. Since then both her parents had been killed in a pileup on an Interstate in California. By the time she had paid for their funeral, there was no money left. For over a year, she had been virtually penniless and homeless, with no one to turn to if Neil decided to come after her.

When she discovered she was pregnant, Lacey had left Denver for St. Louis, reasoning that it was one of the few cities in which Neil had no influential connections. Later, she had deliberately chosen to make her home in this small town in southern Illinois. It was the last place he would look for her. This was where he'd grown up, the town he had left at eighteen to make his way in the world he already viewed with cynical eyes. His painful memories of this place would guarantee that he wouldn't return here, she'd thought, and as the years slipped away she was proved right. She'd been safe... until now.

For a desperate second or two her brain tried to deny the proof in front of her: it must be another Neil Hartmann; he surely wasn't the only man in the world with that name. But a calm, quiet voice inside her rejected the idea at once. It was her Neil all right, and once she'd accepted that fact she took a deep breath, feeling a curious mixture of dread and relief. It was suddenly clear to her that she had always known this day would come. It was inevitable that she would face him again, confronting the ghosts of her past. At least now she could do it from a position of strength, and for that she was thankful. He had once stripped her of everything—pride, self-respect, a home, and her reputation. He had thrown her out with only the clothes she was wearing, two hundred fifty dollars and a wallet full of credit cards he knew she wouldn't dare use.

Lacey looked around her office and was comforted by what she saw. Through her own efforts she had gained back her self-respect, and there was no way he could take it from her again. She slowly placed the paper with his name on it under a bronze paperweight she'd received from the Chamber of Commerce for her leadership in the downtown renewal project. It was only a matter of time. Any day now, he would walk into this office and back into her life. And when he did, she would be ready.

It happened sooner than she'd expected. Vi and Ellen left at four-thirty, their usual time, still laughing about Royal Sawyer's latest request. Lacey stayed on to do the necessary research for that policy. What would he think of next, she wondered, smiling.

As long as there was someone in the office, the front door was never locked, and she looked up in faint irritation an hour later when the soft "ping" of the electronic sensor told her someone had come in. Now what? It had already been a long day, and she wanted to get through the rest of this paperwork before she had to pick up the boys. She started to rise from behind her desk, then froze as a deep male voice called a question from the outer office.

"Anybody here?"

For the last hour Lacey had blocked all thoughts of Neil, but the unforgettable sound of his voice brought a rush of panic, making her knees go weak and her stomach lurch sickeningly. She quickly got a grip on herself and took a deep, steadying breath before walking to the door, fiercely reminding herself that he no longer held the power to hurt her.

He was in partial silhouette, half turned toward the clock on the wall as he checked it against his watch. When he caught her movement from the corner of his eye, he turned, and their gazes locked.

Despite having been forewarned by Ellen's message and having heard his voice, Lacey reacted initially with shock when she saw him. He looked twenty years older, instead of eight. The thick hair she remembered as being an attractive mix of salt and pepper was now a solid gunmetal gray, and there were deep grooves chiseled from his nose to the corners of his mouth and between his shaggy eyebrows. They, at least, were still black, she noticed. He was thinner, too, by at least twenty pounds, and instead of the burnished mahogany complexion she remembered, there was an unhealthy pallor to his skin. He looked *ill*, she realized in amazement. She could never remember his being ill; he refused to even admit to having headaches like everybody else. He was watching her, his unusual eyes registering first a blank bewilderment and then incredulous shock.

"Lacey?"

He said her name hesitantly, his voice little more than a hoarse whisper.

She forced a cool smile to her lips. "Hello, Neil."

There, it was done. She had come face to face with him, and she hadn't fainted or gone into hysterics or fled in terror. Her breath came a little easier as she stood to one side in the doorway. "Why don't you come into my office. I'm the only one here right now."

He seemed frozen, utterly stunned, and she realized that Ellen must not have mentioned her name over the phone. Incredible as it seemed, he apparently hadn't known she was here. It gave her the advantage, and she decided to use it before he somehow managed to wrest it away from her.

"Coffee?" she offered as she turned to reenter her office. She didn't wait to see if he would follow.

She was pouring two mugs of coffee from the drip machine when the fluorescent ceiling fixture threw his shadow across the cabinet and up the wall almost to the ceiling. Resisting the urge to move away from him, she turned and held out one of the brown mugs. He hesitated before taking it, and as she started to move toward her desk his free hand came out to fasten on her arm.

Lacey looked up. Even in her heels, he topped her by several inches, she saw confusion and uncertainty mirrored in his eyes. She glanced pointedly at his restraining hand, watching his fingers tighten a fraction, as if to assure himself that she was real and not just a figment of his imagination. But when she pulled away he let her go, and Lacey hid her relief. For just an instant, when the pressure of his hand increased, fear had spiraled through her.

"I understand you're interested in the Miller property," she said with an air of cool politeness and professional interest, putting the desk between them to settle gracefully into her upholstered swivel chair.

"You knew I was here." It was a flat statement, quietly spoken, but Lacey sensed a challenge, almost an accusation, behind the words as he lowered his long frame into the chair across the desk.

She tried not to be rattled by his tone and the intent way he was staring at her, as if she'd suddenly appeared before him in a puff of smoke. She supposed it was a pretty fair analogy, at that.

"One of my secretaries told me about your call when I got back to the office this afternoon," she told him, still polite but businesslike, and watched surprise flicker across his lean face.

"*One* of your secretaries?"

"Yes. There are two. I own this business," she added in clarification.

She was well satisfied when his surprise turned momentarily to amazement and then to a guarded sort of respect. Lacey forced herself to endure his continued scrutiny without blinking or looking away. How often had he turned that cool, assessing gaze on her in the past? He had the knack of concealing every thought or emotion behind an impassive mask, while those unusual, all-seeing eyes made her feel laid bare to the bone. But although that look had intimidated her before, now it did not. She picked up her mug and took a slow sip of coffee, her eyes never breaking contact with his, her hands steady, and she saw his mouth lift slightly at one corner.

"I see." He smiled, then sipped from his own mug. "Have you been here all along?"

"Almost—for the past six years. Did you come to discuss the Miller farm?"

She could see that her cool composure irritated him. His eyes glinted and his mouth thinned as he banged the mug down on her desk.

"Forget about the Miller farm!" The sudden harshness in his voice didn't surprise Lacey; she'd expected it, been waiting for it. She shrugged and rose from behind the desk.

"I didn't really expect you'd be seriously interested," she said calmly. "That place isn't quite up to your usual standards. But if you'd like to look through our other listings—"

Before she could finish he was around the desk, his fingers digging into the flesh of her upper arms, his face tight with anger.

"How can you sit across a desk from me and act like I'm just another potential customer!"

Lacey met his blazing eyes without flinching. Her voice was cold with contempt when she answered, "Because that's all you are."

His hands tightened convulsively. "Lacey, for heaven's sake...." His voice was thick, the words choked as he abruptly lowered his head to her.

Lacey panicked. His hands, his voice, the glittering intent in his eyes, all instantly transported her back to the last time he'd touched her, almost eight years ago. With a vicious wrench, she broke away from him, putting the width of the room between them.

"Don't touch me, Neil! Don't you ever touch me again!"

One of his hands jerked as if to reach out for her, but then he dropped it to his side. His face once more assumed it's hard, inscrutable mask.

"All right. Why did you come here, Lacey? Why here?"

With some distance between them, she regained most of her composure. "I thought it would be the one place you wouldn't think to look for me," she answered flatly.

Neil's lips compressed as her words sank home, and then he pushed his hands into the front pockets of his slacks with a heavy sigh.

"We have to talk."

"There's nothing to talk about. Nothing, Neil!" she repeated emphatically. "I don't know why you came back here, and frankly I don't care. But it has nothing to do with me."

A frown flickered across his face. "If you mean because I didn't know you were here, that's true. But now—"

"Now, nothing! You just happened to stumble across me after eight years. Don't think that gives you any rights, Neil. It doesn't!"

It was an effort to keep her voice steady. The bitterness of all those years was pushing up inside her, but Lacey was afraid of what might happen if she gave vent to it. The memory of how violent he could be was still strong enough to make her stomach knot in apprehension.

"If I'd known you were here, I'd have come long ago," Neil retorted, his voice tight.

The muscles in Lacey's throat contracted sharply at what she took to be the threat behind those words. "You think I don't know that?" she asked bitterly. "I told you, Neil, that's why I picked this place to live. I've built a life here, a whole new life, a good life."

"And there's no room in it for me—is that what you're saying?" he asked harshly.

"That's exactly what I'm saying, Neil." Her voice

shook slightly, but it was with anger, not fear. The fierce answering glitter in his copper-colored eyes told her he'd read the emotion accurately.

"Damn it, Lacey, you're still my wife!" he said between clenched teeth.

"That's an unfortunate situation, which can be easily remedied," she retorted coldly.

He sucked in his breath, and for one panic-stricken moment Lacey saw rage narrow his eyes. Then he visibly forced himself under control, his hands balling into fists at his sides.

"Are you involved with somebody else—some other man?" he demanded in a barely controlled voice.

"That's none of your business, Neil," she told him calmly, confident that he wouldn't dare do anything to her here. She wanted to show him she wasn't as easily intimidated as she'd been eight years ago. Still, when he took a step toward her, it was all she could do to keep from backing away. But she stood her ground defiantly. She wouldn't back into a corner like a frightened child! She wouldn't give him the satisfaction!

"Lacey, I asked you a question." His voice had gone dangerously soft. "Is there another man in your life?"

Hysterical laughter bubbled up inside her as the twins' faces flashed across her mind.

"Not just one," she said without thinking, and saw his face whiten with anger and shock.

"You've changed," he muttered in harsh accusation.

"You think so?" Lacey retorted. "Considering what you once accused me of, you shouldn't be surprised, Neil. You surely didn't think a little tramp like me would have spent the past eight years living like a nun? Or maybe you thought I'd never be able to tolerate a man's touch after you finished with me? Sorry to disappoint you, Neil," she said with a derisive little smile, "but you didn't *quite* manage to kill the woman in me."

He turned away so she couldn't see his face. "Lacey," he began huskily, "about that night—"

"*No!*" It came out choked with anger. "I won't talk about that. Not now, not ever!"

Neil turned to her again, his face once more stoic and unreadable. "Yes," he said with typical arrogance, "we certainly *will* talk about it. But not here. Get your purse. I'll take you to dinner."

Lacey bit back her furious reply and gave him a cool little smile as she shook her head. "I'm afraid I'll have to refuse your charming invitation, Neil. I'm having dinner with two soccer players tonight."

"Three."

Lacey turned toward the door in surprise. Paul was standing there, looking relaxed and completely at ease in shorts and sweat-dampened T-shirt that read: "Soccer . . . it's a kick in the grass." How long had he been there, she wondered as he grinned lazily.

"I invited myself," he added when she just stood staring at him. "We voted to have pepperoni pizza." His eyes flashed reassurance as he said, "We were just on the way to order it."

Lacey felt her taut muscles suddenly go slack. She

had no idea how much he'd heard, but he'd apparently decided to pretend ignorance of the highly charged atmosphere and the scene he'd just interrupted. The boys must be waiting in his car, and a shuddering relief made Lacey's throat go dry as she realized he could have brought them inside with him.

"Do you want extra peppers?" Paul asked casually, giving her an extra couple of seconds to collect herself.

"Don't I always?" she replied lightly. Then inspiration struck, and she went to pick up her purse and withdraw her house key. "I'm almost finished here. Why don't you go on to the house, and I'll meet you there."

When Paul came to take the key, she saw the puzzled question in his eyes. They flicked to Neil, standing stony faced and rigidly silent beside Lacey's desk, and his mouth curled in an apologetic smile. "I hope I have not interrupted anything important?"

It was clear he expected her to introduce them. Lacey's voice and manner were stiff as she did, and Paul's nod had a look of satisfaction as he offered his hand. For a moment Lacey thought Neil would refuse to take it, but then he did. From the look on his face, she pitied Paul's poor fingers.

"An unusual coincidence, yes?" Paul's accent could have been cut with a knife as he gave her an innocent smile. "That you both should have the same name." He unexpectedly leaned over to kiss Lacey lightly on the cheek and warned her that if she took too long getting home she might not get any pizza, and then left.

After he'd gone the tension in the room grew palpably. Lacey quickly tidied the papers on her desk, then switched off the lamp. She had no intention of staying in the same room with Neil any longer than she had to. Taking her car keys from her purse, she looked up to find him watching her, his eyes hooded.

"What's the asking price for the Miller property?" he asked abruptly.

Lacey's mouth fell open in surprise. "Sixty-five thousand. But don't try to tell me you're actually considering—"

"I'll have a certified check on your desk first thing in the morning," he said curtly, then turned on his heel and strode out of her office.

2

"HE IS the boys' father, isn't he?"

They were in the family room downstairs, sipping Chianti. Paul lounged on the sofa, and Lacey sat with her legs drawn under her on a plump floor cushion. He had waited until the pizza had been eagerly devoured, then waved to them as the twins pedalled their bikes up the block to a friend's house. Now that they were alone, he brought up the subject that had been on both their minds.

Lacey's smile was wry. "You saw him. If I denied it you'd know I was lying. Yes, he's their father, but he doesn't even know they exist."

Paul frowned at her. "How can that be?"

She sighed. Of course he was curious, just as a lot of people would be curious if Neil really intended to buy the Miller farm. That had been worrying her ever since he'd walked out of the office. He never did anything without a reason, but try as she might, she couldn't begin to guess at what would make him buy a rundown farm miles from town.

"Lacey?" Paul's voice intruded on her thoughts, and she turned to him in resignation.

"When we...separated, I was pregnant, but neither of us knew it," she explained, then smiled again at the expurgated version of the story. Put like that, it sounded almost romantic.

Paul leaned forward, his wineglass held in both hands. "But you had parted badly, in anger, and you didn't want him to know," he surmised accurately. Lacey nodded and sipped at her wine. "But Todd and Scott are seven now. In all this time, have you never considered telling him he is a father?"

"Never!" Then, because she realized how harsh and bitter that had sounded, she shrugged and added, "We weren't in contact with each other. Until today, I hadn't seen or spoken to him in almost eight years."

Paul's eyes narrowed in shrewd speculation. "And now you are wishing he had not come back into your life at all," he said softly. "What did he do to you, Lacey, to make you hate and fear him so much?"

"I don't hate him, and I certainly don't fear him!" she denied quickly. She frowned and made a vague gesture with her glass. "There's no reason to be afraid of him now."

The last word told a whole story in itself she realized, and instantly wished it unsaid. But it was too late. Paul's gaze softened in concern as he joined her on the floor. He set his glass on the cocktail table and quite easily and naturally slipped an arm around her shoulders to draw her against him. He wasn't making a pass, Lacey knew, just offering comfort and support. Whether it was the strain of seeing Neil again, or the wine, or both, she suddenly needed what he was offering. She let her head settle on his shoulder gratefully.

"He hurt you badly, didn't he?" Paul asked softly.

"He nearly destroyed me," she answered, and was surprised at how calm her voice sounded.

"Can you tell me?" he murmured close to her ear.

Lacey shook her head. "No. If you're my friend, you won't ask, Paul."

He hugged her shoulders briefly. "All right. Did he divorce you, or was it the other way around?"

Lacey gave a short, cynical laugh. "Neither. He wouldn't—it would be an admission of failure, and he never fails at anything. And I couldn't. If I'd filed a divorce petition, he'd have found out where I was, and I was terrified he might come after me. I lived like a criminal for years, Paul, hiding out, scared half to death he'd find out about the boys and try to take them away from me. *Try?*" she repeated bitterly. "He wouldn't have just tried, he'd have done it. He has the money and the high-priced legal talent, and at that time he'd have done anything to hurt me."

Paul frowned again, but didn't comment on the fact that she'd just informed him she was still a married woman. "But, Lacey," he said on a note of anxiety, "if you never divorced him, mightn't he still try to take them? If he is as ruthless and vengeful as you say—"

"No," she said with conviction. "I'm not a scared girl anymore, Paul. I'm a successful businesswoman, a respected member of this community. I could prove in any court of law that I can provide for them as well as or better than he could, and if he dared to question my fitness as a mother, I could come up with plenty of witnesses on my behalf. He's shrewd enough to see all that. Neil Hartmann doesn't take on lost causes. Still," she murmured on a sigh, "I'd rather he didn't even know about the boys. He might make trouble, and I don't want to see them hurt. Oh *damn*, why did he have to come back here?"

"Did you ask him that?"

Lacey looked up with a regretful smile. "Somehow I didn't think of it. But I will, if he really shows up with a check for the Miller farm in the morning. I can't quite see Neil in a pair of bib overalls."

BUT HE DID SHOW UP, check in hand, at nine-thirty the next morning. Ellen showed him into Lacey's office with a triumphant grin, then closed the door on her way out. *Probably so she and Vi can indulge in some speculation without being overheard*, Lacey thought as Neil casually seated himself. He flicked the check across the desk at her, but Lacey didn't pick it up.

"So you're really serious about buying," she remarked with open skepticism.

"Good morning. It's nice to see you again, too." Neil grinned as he leaned back and crossed his legs, "Have lunch with me today. We'll drive out to that lounge on Highway 1."

His lazy assurance rankled Lacey. He looked as self-confident as ever, sitting there in an oyster-colored string-knit sweater and camel slacks, his feet shod in soft brown moccasins. If anything, the gray hair made him even more distinguished-looking, and the weight loss she'd noticed yesterday emphasized the strong planes and angles of his face. His unusual copper-hard eyes regarded her with a gleam of amusement as she finished her silent inventory.

"I'd be glad to peel down and let you check out the rest, but you'll have to lock the door," he said in a mocking drawl.

Blood rushed to Lacey's cheeks, but the stare she leveled at him was cold enough to give him a case of frostbite. "I've got a better idea. I'll step outside, and let Ellen and Vi come in to view your strip show. I'm sure they'd both appreciate your...maturity much more than I would." Her eyes lifted to his hair as she smiled the last sentence.

Neil's lips twitched in amusement. "Mmm, well, I guess some of us age more gracefully than others. You, for instance. You're more beautiful than ever, Lacey. You really...*really* look good."

His voice dropped on the last sentence, taking on a husky, deliberately sensual timbre. He'd always had a very seductive voice, Lacey remembered. It was deep and resonant, with an almost musical cadence at times that should have been incongruous, but wasn't. But if he thought he could seduce her with that sexy bedroom voice, he had another think coming.

"Why, thank you, Neil," she murmured with a bland little smile, then followed through while he was still grappling with her apparent immunity. "Tell me, just out of curiosity, what the *hell* are you doing here?"

Surprise replaced puzzlement in his eyes, while his features retained their impassivity. And then a smile slowly lifted the corners of his mouth. If his voice was seductive, his mouth was an outright invitation. She'd forgotten how tempting that mouth could be when he let it relax and soften! Lacey tore her gaze from his full lower lip and fought down the memory of how it had felt to have him love her with his mouth.

"Well, well," he murmured softly. "I do believe you've grown up."

"Oh, definitely. Are you going to answer my question?"

He shrugged negligently, but the smile remained in place. "At the moment I'm buying a piece of real estate and waiting for you to accept my invitation to lunch, not necessarily in that order."

"Why?" Lacey insisted. She was beginning to lose patience with his pretense of good fellowship. Who did he think he was kidding? He was so laid-back it was ludicrous! The words "leisure" and "relaxation" weren't part of Neil Hartmann's vocabulary. He was the original workaholic—he didn't know *how* to relax. So just who did he think he was kidding?

"Why?" he repeated with lazy amusement. "Do I need a reason to ask my own wife to lunch?"

"Stop it!" Lacey said with quiet anger. "Just stop it, Neil. If you want to play games to amuse yourself while you're in town, go find somebody else. I have neither the time nor the inclination to indulge your whims."

His smile disappeared. "I'm not playing games, Lacey," he said softly. "And you *are* my wife."

Their eyes locked in a silent battle of wills. Lacey was determined not to lose her temper. If she showed any loss of control, however slight, he would take it as a sign of weakness, and she would be vulnerable to attack.

"Only for the time being," she granted quietly at last.

She was stunned by his reaction. He leaned forward, his eyes suddenly hard and his lean body taut with anger.

"Till death us do part," he said clearly and coldly. "That's the second time in as many days you've made that nasty little threat. No divorce, Lacey. There won't be any divorce."

For a moment she was too stunned and dismayed to reply. Then she leaned back in her own chair and ran her eyes over him contemptuously. *Fight fire with fire*, she told herself firmly.

"Open your eyes, Neil. This is the 1980s. If I decide to divorce you, there's not a damn thing you can do about it. All I have to do is claim irreconcilable differences. It's not even called divorce anymore. The courts refer to it as 'dissolution of a marriage,' and it's almost as simple as renewing your driver's license. I wouldn't even have to show up. My attorney could handle the whole thing for me while I stayed here and ran my business."

"I'd fight it," he spat at her. "If you tried to divorce me, I'd fight you all the way, Lacey."

"Please yourself," she answered with forced calmness. "When one partner wants to end a marriage and the other doesn't, the court usually agrees that they *have* irreconcilable differences." She allowed a small smile to touch her lips. "As I said, Neil, there isn't a damned thing you could do about it. And once a judge heard the sordid history of our marriage, I somehow doubt he'd press very hard for counseling."

She'd expected him to explode and was poised to spring for the door at the first move from him. She wasn't prepared for his tight-lipped silence, or the way he sank back in his chair and raked an agitated hand through his thick hair. A look of bitter defeat clouded his eyes before he closed them with a sigh.

"I knew you'd hate me, but I never imagined just how much," he said dully. "So you've made up your mind."

An actual physical pain speared Lacey's chest, and she was at a loss to understand its cause. It couldn't be the thought of ending something that had to all intents and purposes been over for eight years, she told herself. It certainly couldn't be the sight of Neil looking so...ill, she thought again, and was once more surprised. But yes, he did look ill, and unutterably tired.

"I haven't made any decision about divorce," she said, and the huskiness in her voice was yet another surprise. "To be honest, I hadn't seriously considered it until yesterday. I just want you to realize it's a possibility, Neil, and that *if* I decide it's what I want, you won't be able to bully or coerce me into changing my mind. Now—" she took a deep breath, then let it out slowly "—will you please stop fencing with me and tell me why you've come back here after all these years, and why you're buying a rundown farm in the middle of nowhere? You must realize it will cost you at least as much as you're paying for the property to fix it up?"

His eyes slowly opened, and his mouth twisted in a wry smile. "More. I estimate I'll have to sink another seventy thousand into that place before it's fit to live in."

"But *why*?" Lacey exclaimed. "It isn't like you to throw away your hard-earned capital on something that'll never show a profit, and I can't believe you're buying on impulse. You drove out and saw the place—you know how isolated it is and the condition the buildings are in. The well's contaminated, one of the storage sheds collapsed last winter, and it's a wonder the others haven't given in to gravity before now. You could drive a truck through some of the cracks in the barn walls, and the house, the *house* is. . . ."

"Are you trying to talk yourself out of a sale?" Neil suddenly smiled. He was once more lounging in the chair, the amusement back in his eyes as he lifted one shaggy brow at her.

Lacey flushed, irritated with herself for her lack of professionalism. "I never misrepresent a piece of property. If a buyer feels he's been deceived, he tends to be dissatisfied. And that's bad for business," she added sternly.

"I assure you, Lacey, I'm perfectly satisfied with both the property and the selling price," Neil drawled. "Why don't you think of this purchase as an investment in my future? The older I get, the more I find myself looking back," he reflected. "I've been thinking I'd like to retire here. . . someday."

The last word was added after a split second's hesitation.

"Retire!" Lacey scoffed. "You'll never retire, Neil. You'd be climbing the walls inside a week if you tried. All that peace and quiet would drive you crazy, and you know it."

"You never know what you can put up with until you try," he murmured. Suddenly leaning forward, he captured her left hand as it rested on the desk. "You still wear your rings. I figured you'd have thrown them away years ago."

Lacey resisted the urge to withdraw her hand; there was no telling how he'd construe such a gesture. She wore the rings for the twins' sake. It was bad enough that they had to grow up without a father around; she couldn't add to their problems by refusing to even acknowledge that they had one. In addition to their own natural curiosity, there had been questions from friends and schoolmates over the years. She'd dealt with them by telling the boys that she and their father had separated before they were born, and he lived too far away to visit. So far the explanation had been enough, but she knew the day was coming when they would demand to know more.

"They're much too valuable to throw away," she replied when Neil showed no inclination to release her hand.

His eyes lifted from the rings to her face, his expression guarded. "Valuable," he repeated softly. "You're talking about their monetary value, of course. I don't expect you attach any sentimental value to them. Now I, on the other hand...." He paused as he held up his own left hand for her to see that he still wore the plain gold band she'd slipped on his finger more than ten years ago. "Romantic fool that I am, I feel a ridiculous attachment to this symbol of our eternal love."

Lacey nearly choked at his hypocrisy. "Love!" she replied scornfully. "You don't know the meaning of the word, Neil. The closest you've ever come to experiencing love is the thrill you get closing a multimillion-dollar deal. You're incapable of the real thing, just as you're incapable of trust or faith. Don't talk to me about *love*! I gave you love once. When I think of how I worshipped you—adored you! Fool that I was, I'd have been willing to *die* for you! And what did I get in return for all that pathetically shameless love? Kindness? Consideration? Even pity for the childish way I worshipped at your feet? No, you returned my love with deliberate, sadistic cruelty. You killed it, Neil—butchered it, and then turned your back and walked away."

By the time she finished, she was shaking, and her cheeks were wet with tears of bitterness and remembered pain. Yet a small, isolated part of her was stunned and appalled by her own emotional outburst. She didn't notice that Neil had gone white.

"Lacey, don't!" he said hoarsely, and then he was bending over her hand, pressing his forehead to it. His shoulders rose and fell with his harsh, uneven breathing as he fought for control. Lacey was still too distraught to fully comprehend the effect her diatribe had had on Neil until his ragged voice ended the thick silence in the room.

"It took me about three hours to realize you hadn't done what Jason accused you of," he muttered. His eyes, darkened by emotion, now sought hers, and his lean fingers had her hand in a death grip.

Lacey was nearly blinded by rage. She yanked furiously to free her hand, but he held it fast. "Just which accusation are you referring to?" she choked out. "His claim that I plotted with him to steal your damned formula or the one that had me hopping in and out of his bed? Which charge did you generously acquit me of, Neil?"

"*Both!*" His voice was as strangled as hers. "Both, Lacey! I—" He suddenly broke off, releasing her to get to his feet, turning away as if he didn't want her to see his face.

"When I left the apartment that night, I was still too hurt and angry to think straight," he continued in a rough voice. Lacey nearly laughed. *Hurt?* she thought. *Oh, that's rich. Tell me another one, Neil.* "I felt betrayed. That's the only way I know how to explain it. I stopped at the first bar I came to and threw a fifty at the bartender. I told him when that was gone to let me know, and I'd give him another one."

"I guess I should feel flattered that you gave *me* more than you spent on booze," Lacey remarked acidly. "Two hundreds and a fifty—that's what you stuffed in my purse. As much as any high-priced whore you'd ever had was worth, you said. Only I didn't earn it, did I, Neil?"

"Please, stop!" Neil whirled to face her, and the anguished plea in his eyes turned the rest of her accusing words to dust in her mouth.

"If you never believe another thing I say to you, Lacey, believe this," he said with a fierce intensity. 'When I left that bar I went straight back home. It was the hardest thing I'd ever done in my life, because I knew I'd have to face you after—" His mouth contorted in self-loathing, and then he controlled it and went on.

"By then I'd realized that Jason had lied to protect himself. I was ready to go down on my knees to you, to beg you to try and forgive me." He hesitated, then added in a hollow voice, "But you'd already gone. I nearly went crazy. I was scared to death you might . . . ." He didn't finish, but Lacey knew what he was going to say.

"I thought about it," Lacey whispered, reliving that night when she'd wandered the streets in a daze after leaving their apartment—the apartment he'd ordered her out of before he left.

"Lacey?"

She looked up to find him standing before her, his hands in his pockets and his feet braced apart. He looked very intimidating, and Lacey shivered involuntarily. His mouth tightened when he saw it.

"I want to know whether you believe me," he said quietly.

Lacey sighed. "Does it matter, after all this time?"

He momentarily lost the control he'd regained. "Of course it matters!" he said harshly. Then he astounded her by dropping onto one knee and taking both her hands in his. "Lacey, don't you see, it's important that you believe me. If—"

"*I* wanted to be believed eight years ago, Neil!" she

interrupted. "I *begged* you to believe me, but you took the word of an admitted thief over that of your own wife. You *wanted* to think the worst of me!"

"No!" He'd gone pale again, and his fingers tightened in a bone-crushing grip. "You mustn't think that! I didn't want to believe it, but Jason—"

"The point is, you *did* believe it, Neil. You couldn't have done what you did, otherwise. It might sound crazy, but *that* hurt even more than what you did to me. That you'd actually think me capable of the things Jason accused me of made me sick inside. I knew you didn't love me, but I thought you at least respected me, trusted me."

"I loved you, Lacey." His voice was low and tinged with resignation, "I may not have been able to show you the right way or tell you, but I always loved you. But I guess you don't believe that, either."

After a moment he released her hands and rose to his feet with a lithe, easy grace. His voice was soft, but there was a steely determination in his eyes.

"I've got a lot to atone for, I know. Maybe I can never make it all up to you, Lacey, but I want to try. All I ask is that you give me a second chance."

She stared up at him in disbelief. "Neil...." Her voice began as raspy and weak, but grew stronger as the shock wore off. "You can't be asking me for a reconciliation? Even *you* don't have that much gall!"

His smile was cynical and without humor. "You know better than that, Lacey," he drawled.

Hot color flooded her face. "You think you can just walk back into my life, say, 'I'm sorry, Lacey,'

and expect me to welcome you with open arms? Forget it, Neil!" she snapped. "I'm not buying!"

His sigh sounded more impatient than anything
else. "This isn't working out at all like I planned it."
He grimaced. "I was going to take you to lunch—"

"I wouldn't have gone," Lacey told him flatly.

Neil frowned at the interruption, then continued
as if it hadn't happened. "And soften you up with a
bottle of good wine. Then, when you were feeling
relaxed and mellow, I was going to turn on the
charm."

Lacey's disgusted snort brought a wry smile to his
mouth.

"I think things started to go wrong when I offered
to strip, and you told me in so many words that you
weren't attracted to senior citizens."

Lacey found herself fighting back a smile. This was
a Neil she'd never seen before: self-deprecating, droll,
with a laconic wit she'd never even guessed at.

"Tell me," she murmured dryly, "just when did
you make these grandiose plans?"

"Yesterday, as soon as I got over the urge to find
your house and beat the hell out of that pint-sized
Romeo. When did you develop this disgusting weakness for jocks, anyway?"

"Paul isn't a jock. He's an engineer with degrees
from three universities in two different countries."

Neil grunted to show how impressed he was. "He's
just a shrimp."

"He's five foot ten—almost four inches taller than
me." By now Lacey found it almost impossible not to
grin. This disgruntled old grouch was so far removed

from the Neil Hartmann she'd known that it was hard to believe he was the same man.

"Are you sleeping with him?"

The question caught her by surprise, but only for a moment. Then she realized he'd been leading up to it all along and cursed herself for a fool as she stood up to face him.

"Where do you get off asking me that?" she demanded furiously. "Whether I sleep alone or with the entire male population of this town, it's no concern of yours!"

"All right, all right!" Neil held his hands up in front of him. "Take it easy. I get the message. I forfeited my right to ask that kind of question eight years ago." Then he shrugged carelessly. "I just wanted to know how much competition I'll be up against, that's all."

"You won't be up against *any* competition," Lacey snapped, "because you're not in the running. Get that through your head, Neil! I'd have to be some kind of masochist to want to pick up where we left off."

His eyes took on an opaque sheen, concealing whatever emotion her words sparked in him.

"I guess I deserved that," he said flatly. "I didn't think it would be easy. But if you'll remember, Lacey, once I set my mind to something, I don't quit until the job's done."

"Is that what I am—a job?" she asked scornfully.

A smile briefly touched his firm mouth. "The most difficult one I've ever taken on, from the looks of it," he drawled. Then he unconsciously echoed her thoughts of a few minutes earlier. "I'd almost swear you're not the same person."

"I'm not," Lacey assured him. "I was a foolishly naive girl then. Now I'm a woman who knows her own mind. And who knows you for what you are," she added scathingly.

That brought a flicker of reaction to his eyes before he turned for the door. He stopped with his hand on the knob to look back at her.

"I have to go back to Denver to finalize a deal, but as soon as that's out of the way I'll have some free time. I should be back around the middle of next week. I'll come in to take care of the closing costs on the farm then. That should give you plenty of time to organize your defense."

"I don't need a defense against you!" Lacey snapped.

Neil smiled slowly and let his eyes run over her, from her hair to her toes and back again, taking his time. "Oh, yes you do," he said softly. And then he left, before she could overcome her inarticulate rage and get in the last word.

Lacey looked down at the check on her desk and was tempted to rip it into tiny pieces. What kind of sick game was he playing, she wondered. He'd have some free time, and he thought he could amuse himself by tormenting her. Well, just let him try! Her mouth set into a grim line as she took the rubber stamp from the desk and endorsed the check, smearing the ink in her anger.

3

"BEAUTIFUL PASS, SCOTT! Now go for it, Todd! Don't hesitate, charge ahead!"

It was Saturday afternoon, and Paul was shouting encouragement to his star players from the sidelines. He turned briefly to Lacey, his expression excited and baffled at the same time.

"Did you see that? They *must* use some form of telepathy—there is just no other explanation!"

He paused to laugh and shake a jubilant fist in the air when Todd neatly spiked the ball past a surprised goalie and into the net, then gave her his attention once more.

"So, did you find out why their father has suddenly turned up out of the blue?"

"He *says* he intends to retire here, and that's why he's buying the farm," Lacey answered.

Paul frowned and pursed his lips. "He seemed much too vital a man to be thinking of retirement, though I suppose he must be old enough."

"He's only forty-five," Lacey replied with just a trace of indignation. "And I'm sure retirement's still a long way off. He's just planning ahead."

Paul gave her a keen glance, but didn't comment on her slight defensiveness. They were silent for a while as they watched the soccer practice, Paul now and then yelling directions or criticizing a sloppy play or formation. Lacey stood beside him, frowning slightly, her arms folded across her blue tank top. Finally she asked, "Paul, did you think Neil looked sick when you met him the other day?"

He turned to her in surprise. "Sick? No, I wouldn't say he looked sick. He did seem a little pale, and his features looked drawn—more like a person who is recovering from an illness, I would say. Why? Did he seem unwell to you?"

Lacey shook her head, still frowning. "No, not exactly. He just wasn't acting like himself, and as you said, his color wasn't good. I wouldn't have thought anything of it, except that I remember him as always being disgustingly healthy."

She shrugged as if the subject of Neil's health was unimportant and tried to concentrate on watching Todd and Scott. But that didn't help banish thoughts of her husband—quite the contrary. She couldn't even look at them now without seeing Neil in them—in the way they scowled when one of them made a mistake and lost control of the ball; or the stubborn set of their chins. . . . They even walked like him, she thought, as Paul called a halt to the practice and they strolled over to the sidelines. Neil's confident, rolling gait could almost be called a swagger, and she noticed for the first time that both boys walked exactly the same way. She let her thoughts drift as Paul reviewed the day's practice and announced the time for the next one, knowing her sons would repeat everything he said like parrots in the car on the way home, anyway.

It had been three days since Neil's last visit, and during that time Lacey had grown increasingly tense. He'd be back the middle of next week, he'd said. That gave her roughly four more days to decide whether to tell him he was the father of twin sons.

She was of two minds, torn between the dictates of her conscience and her deep-seated maternal instinct to protect the boys. He had a right to know about them—there was no question about that. It would be selfish not to tell him, to deny him the pleasure of knowing them. Yet at the same time she was afraid, and if she was honest, not just for the twins. Neil had never expressed a wish for children when they were living together and wouldn't have had time to be a good father if they'd had a child. It was entirely possible that he would reject them just as he'd once rejected her. Or worse, he might decide to use them as weapons against her. She believed he was fully capable of using even his own children, if it suited his purposes.

Then, too, there was the unknown factor of how long he intended to stay in town. He'd said he would have "some free time." How much free time, and would he spend all of it here? Doing what—launching an all-out campaign to convince her to give their marriage another try? The thought alone was enough to make Lacey shiver under the warmth of the bright June sun. When Neil Hartmann went after something, he usually got it, and she had the uncomfortable feeling that by standing up to him she'd presented a challenge too tempting to resist. She didn't for a second believe that he actually wanted to resume their marriage. Oh no, it was just the thrill of the chase that excited him, as she'd learned the hard way. Once he got what he thought he wanted, he soon grew bored and lost interest.

Lacey and Paul had a date of a couple of weeks' standing that night. They were going to the country club for dinner, and Mrs. Moore was coming to sit with the boys. As Lacey emerged from a steaming shower, her mind partly occupied with deciding what to wear, it occurred to her for the first time that she was a married woman who made a fairly regular practice of going out with a man other than her husband. She frowned as she selected a clingy bright green Qiana dress from her spacious closet. Should she be feeling guilty . . . ashamed?

"Not one bit!" she muttered with quiet vehemence, flinging the dress onto her bed.

There was absolutely no reason for any guilt on *her* behalf. Her marriage to Neil might still be in effect legally, but in every other way it had ended years ago. And not through any fault of hers! Why should she feel guilty about going out with Paul, enjoying herself a little, when for the past eight years she'd lived the life of a nun while paying for someone else's sins!

She stood wrapped in a towel in the middle of her bedroom floor as that last ugly scene in her office replayed itself on the screen of her mind. Her fists clenched at her sides, her heartbeat accelerating in agitation. Why had she ever opened up those old wounds, put herself through the pain of reliving the horror of that long-ago night?

For a moment hatred toward Jason Trent welled up inside, threatening to choke her. What was he doing now, she wondered resentfully. How had *he* spent the past eight years? Living it up on the money he'd been paid by one of Neil's competitors for the formulas he'd spirited out of the plant? That he'd *stolen* from a man who was an old friend as well as his employer was treacherous enough, but to have been so cowardly as to involve Lacey in the hope of saving his own skin, she found utterly despicable.

Still, she reminded herself grimly, she couldn't lay all the blame for what had happened at Jason's door. No one had put a gun to Neil's head and forced him to believe Jason's incredible story, thrown together on the spur of the moment in a desperate attempt to shield himself. Neil had accepted of his own free will what Jason told him, choosing to believe the man's vile accusations over her tearful, pleading denials. And for that she would never forgive him. *Never!*

She dressed and made up for the date with Paul in a mood of angry defiance, determined to put Neil out of her mind for tonight, at least. He'd caused her enough anguish already, and she *wouldn't* let thoughts of him spoil this evening!

Paul's smile when she opened the front door to him would have been compliment enough, but he supplemented it by remarking softly, "Charming, *cara*, utterly charming. You look far too young and sexy to be the mother of seven-year-old sons."

Lacey's mouth tightened involuntarily as the comment reminded her of her sons' father, but Paul apparently didn't notice. He went with her to say goodbye to the boys in the family room, then took her arm as they strolled out to his dark blue Porsche.

The club dining room was booked to capacity, as it was most Saturday nights. It was a young crowd, and everyone there was known to everyone else. There was a lot of mingling, a lot of table-hopping after dinner, when the lights were lowered and a small combo moved in to provide the music for dancing.

"Will you do me a very large favor?" Paul asked Lacey as he shifted his chair closer to hers to make room for another couple at their table. When the dancing began, about half the tables were usually shoved against one wall to double the amount of floor space.

"Sure...as long as it's not immoral, illegal or fattening," Lacey said with a grin.

He leaned close, his dark eyes glittering and a slight quirk to his mouth as he murmured, "Try to remember that you are here to enjoy yourself—and my company. If someone happens to mention that his house just burned to the ground, tell him to come in to the office tomorrow and you'll settle his claim. But *please*, *cara*, for tonight, no business. Can you manage that, do you think?"

Lacey sipped at her drink to conceal an amused smile. "I'll do my best," she murmured solemnly.

Paul often teased her about her dedication to her career, though she knew that in reality he admired that dedication and respected her for the success she'd achieved. He was really a very pleasant person to spend time with, she thought, as Phil and Sherry Engel pulled chairs up to their table and joined them. Paul was charming, witty, undemanding and secure enough not to feel threatened when they were out together and she started talking business, usually with another man.

It happened again when Phil asked her about a commercial property she'd recently listed, and Lacey had to smile as she caught Paul's comical grimace. After a few minutes she tactfully ended the conversation by claiming the band was playing her favorite song, grabbing his hand and pulling him onto the dance floor.

"Since when is 'Smoke Gets in Your Eyes' your favorite song?" Paul asked as he guided her around the floor with an enviable athletic grace.

Lacey grinned. "Since Phil started dropping hints about how much his property ought to be worth, compared to the lot Ed Weintraub is trying to sell. Besides," she added with a straight face, "I'm here to enjoy myself, not talk business all night."

His arm briefly pressed against her back, and he smiled down at her.

"I'm just thankful his house didn't burn down," he murmured, and Lacey smiled back at him as he spun her around in time to the music.

When they returned to the table Paul seated himself next to Phil and put Lacey beside Sherry, thereby forestalling the possibility of any lengthy conversations in which he wouldn't be an active participant. Lacey realized it was a slightly proprietary move, but it was done with such charm that she somehow couldn't be offended. And besides, he was right. She *should* concentrate on enjoying herself. Heaven knew she didn't go out socially all that often. When she did have a function to attend in the evening, it was usually a meeting of one of the several clubs and organizations to which she belonged. She and Paul rarely saw each other more than once a week, and sometimes not that often.

Still, she thought, when they were together she always knew she'd have a good time. He was really quite a catch: handsome, a good conversationalist, intellectually stimulating, not to mention incredibly virile. In short, Paul was everything any woman would look for in a man.

So why don't I feel more for him, she wondered. *Why don't I get goosebumps when he holds my hand?* Paul made no secret of the fact that he wanted to go to bed with her, and while the thought no longer terrified her as it had in the beginning, neither did it particularly appeal to her. She thought of Paul as a good friend—a very good friend—but it was suddenly clear to her that she didn't want the relationship to develop beyond that stage.

Was it because she was so fond of him and didn't want to risk losing the friendship, the easy companionship they shared? Or was it that deep down inside she still shied away from the thought of physical intimacy with *any* man?

And that, of course, brought her thoughts back to Neil, whom she'd determined not to think about at all tonight.

Oh, damn! she thought in exasperated anger. Was she destined to be haunted by him day and night for the rest of her life? Even here, surrounded by the friends she'd made in her new life, the physical proof of all she'd accomplished since they had parted, he intruded. She resented him for coming back into her life, but at least she no longer feared him, and for that she was deeply grateful. The fear had faded to a constant state of nervous tension—irritating, but bearable. He couldn't hurt her any more, because she wouldn't give him the chance, wouldn't let him get close enough. Oh no, not again.

For the rest of the evening she made a concerted effort to block any stray thought that might open her mind to unpleasant memories or pointless speculation about the future. *Enjoy what you've got while you've got it,* she told herself with sensible practicality, and she tried hard to follow her own advice.

When Paul took her home he stayed for coffee after Mrs. Moore left. That wasn't unusual; they often finished an evening out by unwinding over a cup of cappucino, which he made, and maybe catching the end of "The Tonight Show." What made this night different was that Paul turned off the television and tuned the radio to an all-night classical station instead, then drew her down beside him on the sofa.

"This has all the earmarks of a classic seduction scene," Lacey murmured.

"Would you mind?" His voice was soft, perfectly serious, his eyes solemnly holding hers. "Would you object to being seduced by me, *cara*? You have known for a long time it's what I want—for us to be lovers."

"Yes," Lacey admitted. She frowned, inexplicably

disappointed in him. Yet, it was stupid and immature to feel that way, she knew. She'd always felt the time would come when Paul would want a definite answer one way or the other.

His arm slipped around her shoulders, his fingers feathering against her cheek. "Lacey," he coaxed softly, "I am not an insensitive brute. I understood from the beginning that there was a great anxiety in you about allowing any sort of closeness between us. Since I have never been burdened with an excess of false modesty, I assumed it was not myself you feared and mistrusted but men in general. Now I understand that it was your husband who caused this fear, this mistrust." He sighed, the pressure of his fingers increasing fractionally.

"*Cara*, look at me, please." Reluctantly, she did. His dark gaze had a withdrawn, brooding quality as he studied her face. "I think, to my great regret, that you will never be able to share the best of yourself with me or anyone else until you have finished with him."

"I *have* finished with him," Lacey said, but somehow her voice lacked the necessary conviction.

"No. No, you have not. Not yet." Paul, by comparison, sounded very sure, very confident. "When you have, I will be waiting. It will be well worth the wait, I think," he added almost to himself as his eyes probed hers with an intensity that was almost alarming.

After he left and all the next day, Lacey dwelt on what he'd said and was troubled by it. She had to finish with Neil, Paul claimed. Okay, maybe he was right. And maybe Neil's reentry into her life wasn't a totally negative thing, if it would give her the opportunity to put the past behind her once and for all. She'd already made a good deal of progress toward that end, just by coming face to face with him and surviving intact. That alone said a lot about how much she'd matured during their separation and gave her a new estimation of her own worth, her own emotional stability.

She harbored no illusions about Neil's strength and determination, but at least now she appreciated that she possessed those qualities, too. If he tried to pressure her, she could withstand all he gave, and then some. If what he had in mind was a waiting game, playing on her nerves, she was up to that, too. No matter what tactics he used, she was capable of fighting him and winning; and that belief gave her a new confidence as well as a new peace of mind. She truly doubted that he was serious about resuming their marriage, but she dreaded a future of long, drawn-out battles of wills, more arguments and bitter recriminations and a repeated dredging up of the past. *But if it comes to that,* she told herself, *so be it. I can handle anything he dishes out!*

BY MONDAY EVENING, she'd decided to play things by ear. *If* Neil returned she would first find out how long he planned to stay, and go from there. She would be cool, keeping him at a distance, and hope that once he realized she had no intention of falling into his arms he'd give up and leave her in peace.

As for telling him about the boys, she'd wait and

see. If he was only going to be popping in and out of their lives between business deals, she'd already half decided to hide their existence from him. A father they'd never known was better than one who was likely to disappear overnight, just when they'd grown attached to him. No, they deserved a full-time father, something she couldn't imagine his ever being or even wanting to be.

Tuesday was incredibly hectic. Lacey wished with all her heart that Rick Baker, her one and only full-time salesman, would get himself kicked out of the summer school he was attending and sent back, before she dropped dead of exhaustion. At five-thirty she turned off her desk lamp, rubbing the back of her neck as she collected her purse, and prepared to lock up. Thank goodness this wasn't her week to drive in the car pool. The boys would have been picked up by Elaine Dickens for swim-club practice at four, and would probably arrive home about the same time she did.

She turned off all but the two lights always left on in the outer office as a security measure, and was groping in her purse for her car keys when the door opened and Neil came through it.

Her weary brain was slow to respond. For a moment she just looked at him, taking in his tall form, the casual tan cotton shirt open at the throat to expose a wedge of silver curling chest hair, and finally the tailored brown slacks hugging his lean waist and hips. In the next instant the total effect of all the components hit her like a shock wave, and she nearly reeled. So much for all her carefully considered, confident plans to remain aloof from him, she thought.

Later she would tell herself it was only a combination of surprise, exhaustion and emotional strain that made her react so strongly, but in that moment there was no chance for self-deceit. She knew, with her mind and her body that it was nothing more or less than an involuntary and frighteningly powerful response to his virility. Her sexuality, so long repressed, flared to instant life in recognition and awareness of his, and her body trembled, triggering a chain reaction of memories.

"Neil?" she murmured huskily, sounding dazed.

A slow smile warmed his rugged features as he closed the door behind him. "Hi. Missed me?"

Lacey deliberately ignored that. "I didn't expect you back until tomorrow at the earliest. You said...."

He came forward, his eyes glowing as he took in her flushed cheeks and slight breathlessness. *Please, God, let him think it's just surprise*, Lacey prayed silently as she stood rooted to the spot, unable to tear her eyes from his lean, smiling face. A tendril of fear began to curl through her stomach as she accurately read the look in his eyes.

"I finished up early." His voice was low and even huskier than hers. "I didn't want to be there, anyway. I wanted to be here, with you." He shook his head as he gazed down at her, his eyes tracing her features one by one with unhurried enjoyment, lingering longest on her slightly parted lips.

"All the way back I had this crazy fear that I'd dreamed last week, that you weren't really here, or if you were, that I'd only imagined how beautiful you are," he told her in a throaty murmur. Then one of his hands lifted to her cheek, his fingers lightly following its delicate curve to the corner of her mouth. She saw his eyes darken suddenly, flames leaping in their shadowed depths, and her breath caught in a mixture of fear and excitement. Neil heard it and reached for her.

"Oh, Lacey," he moaned as his arms closed around her, and his mouth closed urgently over hers.

For a moment, she stiffened. Neil's lips instantly softened, his hands becoming gently persuasive as they stroked her slender back, finding the tension between her shoulder blades and soothing it away, his lean fingers warm through the fabric of her blouse.

"Don't be afraid, darling," he whispered against her lips. "Please don't be afraid of me." There was an unexpected tremor in his voice, and she felt it spread to his arms as their pressure increased slightly. "Oh, Lacey, it's been so long," he sighed against her cheek, his breath hot and moist. "Too long. You don't know how I've missed you, *needed* you. Please, darling, just let me—"

His mouth slid over hers again, already open and hungrily seeking a response. When his tongue gently probed her trembling lips, a streak of white-hot fire shot through her, a crackling, lightning flash of desire that made her shudder uncontrollably as her lips parted in mute acceptance.

Neil groaned and his tongue thrust deep, not gently now, but hard and strong, as one hand clasped the back of her head and held it for his invasion. The move was unnecessary. Lacey's hands were already finding their way around his back, then climbing to clutch at his shoulders as her eager tongue met the demand of his and answered with her own. She felt his shoulders tense, and then his arms were contracting, trying to drag her into his body as he plundered the sweet, soft recesses of her mouth.

Lacey's fear had disappeared almost at once, smothered under the instantaneous heat of passion. Even as her mind remembered with painful clarity the punishment he had once inflicted on her, her body ignored that memory and concentrated instead on the mindless joy he could give her—and had given her countless times in the past. His insistent mouth was fast draining her of the ability to reason, and a surging need rose quickly to fill the void, until she was clinging to his shoulders and straining her body against his, striving desperately for a closer contact than their clothes would allow.

"Neil," she gasped when he temporarily left her lips to scatter quick, fervent kisses over her cheeks and closed eyes. "Oh, Neil!"

"*Yes!* He groaned the acknowledgment of a shared hunger into her mouth as he returned to it, his kiss devouring, his appetite seemingly insatiable as his lips ground hers.

"Lacey, I can't believe I've really found you, that you're really here."

His voice was choked, cracking under the intensity of his emotions as his shaking hands ran frantically over her back, clasping her to him and then relaxing to a trembling gentleness, alternating between fierce demand and tender reassurance as he teetered on the thin edge of control.

Lacey felt the immensity of his need and his enormous struggle to hold it in check, and the knowledge fanned the flames of desire already licking at what remained of her own control. Her hands began to move with his, at first hesitantly and then with growing confidence. They caressed his back and lean flanks, skimming over his rib cage and the sharp angle of his shoulder blades. Her fingers rediscovered the width and power of his shoulders, the sheer male strength of him, and itched to do more. Under her increasingly agitated caresses his shirt separated from his pants, and her cool hands encountered warm, smooth flesh, which quivered and contracted at her touch.

Neil gasped his pleasure into her neck. "Lacey, Lacey, you're driving me insane!" he muttered, and the admission spurred her to tease him with her nails, raking them lightly down his sides in a tormenting caress. He was holding her too tightly for her to reach his chest, so she had to content herself with a restless exploration of his back and sides, running her hands aggressively up under his shirt to pull at him, wanting him even closer, craving the exultation that always came with the knowledge that she could affect him as powerfully as he affected her.

This, at least, hadn't changed. Despite all that had happened between them, despite the bitter, lonely years of struggle and hardship, the moment he'd touched her her body had responded with the same swift, consuming passion he'd always been able to arouse. Lost to sensation, Lacey didn't stop to think about the consequences of her deliberately arousing caresses. Years of self-denial had left her starved for the soaring pleasure she knew Neil could give her, and now she moaned softly, a hungry little animal sound that sent a shudder through him when he heard it.

When his shaking hand fumbled with the buttons of her blouse, Lacey didn't stop him. Her breasts were already swollen and hard, nipples stiffly erect as first his lean fingers and then his warm lips joyfully discovered the absence of a bra and took immediate advantage of the fact. Her head fell back, her eyes closed as she felt the first tentative flick of his tongue on her breasts. Her hands came out from under his shirt to clutch at his thick hair, holding him to her, and with a sighing moan Neil's lips closed softly over her breast.

A sweet shaft of pure pleasure pierced Lacey's heart. It felt indescribably right to have him beside her like this, just as his sons had been. She realized that her fingers had relaxed their frantic grip and were now moving softly, lovingly through his hair. She was filled with warmth, soft and melting in his embrace, ready to give whatever he asked and more. This was what she had been made for, to be loved by Neil: Neil's hands, Neil's mouth, Neil's wonderfully hard, strong body.

When his lips deserted her breast for her neck, she murmured a protest and turned toward him, her hands at the back of his head to guide his mouth to hers. Her melting surrender was more than he could take. His kiss hardened to demand as one hand kneaded her breast with a rough urgency and the other slid down her back to pull her hard against him. The throbbing pressure of his arousal against her stomach shocked Lacey into awareness of just how far they had gone and exactly where they were headed. Suddenly his hands seemed cruel instead of urgent, and his rasping breath sounded loud and harsh in her ears. The hard evidence of his desire wasn't a promise but a threat, and terror sprang to life inside her.

"*No!*" she cried as she wrenched her mouth free and tried to wedge her hands between them to shove him away. "Don't . . . please, *please* stop!"

Neil's head shot up, the passion quickly clearing from his eyes when he heard the fear in her quavering voice and felt it in her body. He swore softly but refused to release her, even though Lacey struggled with a strength born of desperation. Instead his arms enfolded her and held her close to his chest, firmly but gently, exerting only as much pressure as was needed to keep her from breaking away from him.

"Shh, it's all right. Easy, baby, it's all right. Relax, I promise I won't do more than hold you. That's all, just hold you."

Slowly his undemanding embrace and soft, deep voice reassured her, and she felt her heart slow its furious pounding and her breathing return to normal. She let her head rest on his shoulder, still shaken and needing a support of some kind, for the moment accepting that it was Neil who provided it.

"Okay now?" he asked after a while, and Lacey nodded, afraid to look up at him. When she felt his lips brush against her temple she shivered, though whether in fear or for some other reason, she couldn't have said.

"I'm sorry, sweetheart," Neil murmured, and there was genuine regret in his voice. "I was afraid that might happen, and I swore to myself that I'd go slow, give you some time."

Lacey did look up then, in surprise. He smiled down at her a little ruefully and then began to calmly and deftly refasten her blouse.

"So much for good intentions," he said dryly. "The second I touched you they flew right out the window. I just couldn't help myself, Lacey. You go straight to my head—always have, always will."

She stared at him in silence. In the two years they'd lived as man and wife, he hadn't once made such an admission, at least not with words. That it was true she didn't doubt for an instant; still held close against his body, she couldn't help but be aware that his desire hadn't abated. But because of that iron control of his—which had often frustrated and angered her, but for which she was now fervently thankful—he could clamp down on his own emotions and talk to her as calmly as if they'd just happened to meet on the street.

"Have I grown an extra nose or something?" he asked soberly, and Lacey blinked before shaking her head.

"It's just...I don't know you anymore," she said huskily, her soft hazel eyes large in her face.

Neil gazed down at her, then a shadow seemed to pass across his eyes.

"Maybe that's good," he said as he lifted a finger to stroke her cheek. "I meant what I said last week, Lacey. I really do want to make a fresh start. I know it won't be easy, but I want us to try, more than I've ever wanted anything in my life." He paused a moment. "If thinking of me as somebody else will help— some stranger you've just met—then that's all right. I'd rather face the past together and put it behind us, but if you can't do that yet, I'll understand. And this kind of thing won't happen again until you're ready. Just to be near you, maybe hold you or kiss you once in a while, that's all I ask for now."

He spoke softly and with undeniable sincerity. He meant every word, Lacey realized in amazement. He was looking at her steadily, his eyes holding a solemn question. She shook her head in uncertainty.

"I don't know, Neil," she told him honestly. "I just don't know. You're asking a lot."

"I know I am. But if we make it, just think, Lacey . . . just think what we stand to gain."

The promise in his eyes was fever bright, compelling her to believe, to have faith that this time they could build something that would last a lifetime. Could they? With everything that stood between them, all the hurt and resentment, might they really have a second chance at happiness? And just as important, did she want to try?

He apparently didn't expect her to make a decision that very minute. His expression softened as he gazed down into her confused, troubled eyes.

"You look beat. Why don't you go on home. We can finish the paperwork for the farm later."

The farm! Lacey had completely forgotten. As they left the building together she noticed the new four-wheel-drive pickup parked next to her Audi.

"It's mine," Neil said before she could ask. "I bought it this morning." Then he grinned. "I figured you've gotta have a truck if you wanta be a farmer."

Lacey was momentarily taken aback. She looked up at him as he opened her car door. "It sounds like you intend to stay around a while," she said cautiously. "I thought you were buying this place as a retirement home."

"I am," Neil answered casually, then completely floored her with his next remark. "I've just sold Hartline, Incorporated, lock, stock and barrel. As of noon this coming Saturday, I'll be officially retired."

Lacey felt as if she'd been punched in the stomach. She drew an unsteady breath, her brain struggling frantically to absorb the full import of what he'd said.

"You mean you're retiring, *now*? And the farm...and the truck...." She trailed off, turning her head to look over his shoulder at the gleaming silver-and-black four-by-four. Neil wasn't the kind of man who indulged himself in expensive toys. He wouldn't have bought it if he didn't intend to use it frequently. Her stomach quivered in nervous apprehension.

"Like I said, what good's a farm without a farm truck?" Then he sobered as he took in her anxious expression. "Yes," he murmured, an almost grim note in his voice. "I intend to take up permanent residence here, Lacey. No running back and forth to Denver or anyplace else. I'll be right here, where I can see you and talk to you and be with you. You might as well make up your mind to it: from now on I intend to be very much a part of your life, whether you like the idea or not. And from the look on your face, it's pretty clear you aren't exactly thrilled."

Lacey's temper flared. "I might have known you hadn't really changed," she blazed. "All that noise about wanting us to try again was just that, wasn't it—*noise!* You'd already made up your mind to move in and take over. To hell with what anybody else wants—Neil Hartmann always gets his own way in the end. You had this all planned before you even left here last week, didn't you? And to think I almost fell for that touching line about making a fresh start! Nothing's changed at all, has it? You're still the same unscrupulous tyrant you always were!"

"Stop it!" He grabbed her by the arms, shaking her angrily. "I meant every word of what I said in there! Why the hell do you think I decided to buy that rundown, overpriced piece of real estate! Yes, all right, I admit I'd made up by mind to move back here before I left last Wednesday. How else was I going to be near my stubborn shrew of a wife?"

Lacey opened her mouth to make a furious retort, but before even one word could pass her lips, his were locked on them in a hard, determined kiss. When he released her she glared at him, her chest heaving.

"You promised not to do that again!" she accused hotly.

"No, I didn't. I told you I'd kiss you once in a

while. I promised not to let things get out of control, and I didn't. And if you'll notice, you're not exactly quaking in fear, either."

"I'm too mad, that's why!" Lacey snapped, and Neil threw back his head with a deep-chested laugh of enjoyment.

"Lacey, you're fantastic!" he claimed when his mirth had subsided. "Courtin' you's gonna be a real pleasure, ma'am."

"I guess it wouldn't make any difference at all if I said I don't *want* to be courted by you?"

Lacey tried hard to maintain her anger, but it was surprisingly difficult. Despite herself, she realized that she was more than a little flattered by his single-minded determination.

Also undeniable was the stimulation she experienced during these verbal sparring matches. In the old days she'd never have dreamed of standing her ground and talking back to him this way, even if he'd given her the chance. But now she enjoyed it. It was exhilarating to see the new respect in his eyes when she gave as good as she got. He was seeing her as an adult for the first time, and she thought he liked what he saw. No, she *knew* he liked what he saw. It was more than just the sexual thing, strong as that still was; it was the surprised but pleased look in his eyes, as if he'd discovered a hidden bonus he hadn't counted on.

Neil leaned an arm on the roof of her car and studied her with those unusual, fascinating eyes. "Don't fight me, Lacey," he advised in a sexily soft murmur. "It won't do any good, and you know it. I realize you're afraid to trust me, believe in me, but you can't deny you're still attracted to me, and that's a beginning. Besides," he added with a glint of humor, "I *owe* you a courtship. When we first met, I was so desperate to get you chained to me that I couldn't spare any time to woo you."

"But now that you've put yourself out to pasture, so to speak, you've got all the time in the world, right?" she muttered, mainly to cover the foolish pleasure she felt at the idea of Neil actually wanting to "woo" her, as he put it. It was true that they'd married in such a rush—barely three weeks after they had met—there hadn't been time for a conventional courtship, but she hadn't wanted to wait any more than he had.

"Right," he agreed easily, his mouth hinting at another grin. "See, there are advantages to having an older lover. I've got both time and money to lavish on you. All I need is the opportunity and your co-operation."

Lacey had never felt more confused in her life. Part of her wanted desperately to believe him, yearned for a real marriage based on mutual trust and respect as well as the physical love they'd always had. But another part whispered that she'd be a fool to give in to temptation, that he would only hurt her again.

4

"Why, Neil?" she asked softly, her hand still on the car door.

"There are two possible explanations," he said gently, smiling. "One is that I need to work off my guilt for what happened before."

"And the other one?"

His smile died. "Give it some time," he murmured. "It'll come to you."

The only other possible explanation for all the trouble he'd gone to was that he was in love with her, but Lacey dismissed that idea at once. A frown marred the smooth line of her brow as she gave a faint shake of her head.

Neil's soft sigh was almost imperceptible. "It looks like I've got my work cut out for me," he told himself under his breath. "Might as well get an early start."

He slowly pulled her into his arms, and Lacey's protest was more surprised than indignant.

"Neil! We're on a public street!"

The rest was smothered as he lowered his head to kiss her with a tenderness that was totally new to her. It was the sweetest kiss she'd ever experienced, completely lacking in passion but with an intense longing that affected her every bit as profoundly.

"Does this tell you anything?" Neil murmured against her lips before he sealed them with another kiss. When he ended it he went on holding her, his cheek pressed to her hair and his hands gently caressing her back.

"Neil?" Lacey asked shakily, and he pulled away a little to look down at her. She was shocked by what she saw in his eyes: pain, and longing. A second later she was telling herself she must have imagined it, as he stood back and replaced his stoic mask of indifference.

"You'd better be going," he said dryly. "I imagine you're seeing one or more of your jocks tonight."

The twins! They'd be home any minute, and no one was there! Lacey completely missed the subtle question in Neil's voice as she hurriedly slid into the car and put her key into the ignition. He closed her door and then leaned down to face her through the open window.

"Enjoy your freedom while it lasts, Lacey," he said grimly. "You've had eight years to play the field, but from now on I intend to be the one and only man in your life."

Play the field! If he only knew, she thought bitterly. Until Paul, she hadn't had one single date since she left him. She'd been too busy raising her sons and trying to keep a roof over their heads, in addition to her revulsion toward any man who even hinted at wanting more than a casual friendship. After Neil, the thought of any kind of intimacy had terrified her for a long time. It was only in the last few months that she'd allowed herself to start thinking in terms of a sexual relationship, and then only because of Paul's dogged persistence.

"You'll never be the *only* man in my life, Neil," she told him brusquely. "Right now I'm going to meet two who mean more to me than you ever did or ever will."

He blanched, and she had the satisfaction of knowing it wasn't only from anger. She had hit him where it hurt, right in that arrogant male ego of his.

"You've changed even more than I thought," he grated. "I guess I'm at least partly to blame for what you've become, Lacey, but don't think you'll turn me off by throwing your other men in my face. I'll just have to work that much harder to prove that I'm the only one for you. And I am. You know it as well as I do."

"All I know is that you're making me late," she told him coolly. "Will you please get your hand off the door so I can leave?"

He hesitated, his eyes narrowing in anger. Lacey's met and held them, refusing to let him intimidate or goad her, and gradually she saw the anger change to a grudging admiration.

"You crafty little witch," he murmured softly. "It won't work, Lacey. You can't freeze me out or protect yourself by hiding behind other men. What on earth do you see in that soccer-playing Romeo, anyway? You're more woman than he could ever handle."

"Is that the voice of experience speaking?" she asked in a bored tone.

"You're damned right it is," Neil answered huskily.

"Even at eighteen, you were the hottest female in bed I'd ever known, and by then I'd known plenty."

Lacey flushed scarlet. "Don't be crude!" she snapped, and Neil chuckled as he stepped back from the car.

"Better hurry, or you'll be late for your date," he taunted softly. "While you're with those other two guys, try not to dwell too much on what it was like with us. A man can always tell when his woman's mind is elsewhere."

LACEY DRESSED FOR WORK the next morning with even more care than usual, torn between anticipation and dread at the prospect of seeing Neil again. As she studied her reflection in the full-length mirror on her closet door, she told herself the anticipation proved beyond any doubt that she definitely had a masochistic streak.

She'd chosen one of the new outfits she'd bought on holiday in Florida, a gauzy shirtwaist dress in rose pink with rolled sleeves and a slender skirt. The skirt was lined but the bodice wasn't, which meant she'd had to buy a satin bra in the same shade of pink. In Denver or St. Louis she'd have gotten by with going braless, as she usually did, but this was a small town in the middle of the conservative Midwest, and she couldn't risk offending customers or potential customers with a lewd display of her breasts.

"Not bad, old girl," she told her reflection as she turned sideways to check that the hem fell evenly.

Lacey had the body of a woman ten years younger, a fact she was aware of without feeling vain. If she was obsessive about anything at all, it was the importance of diet and exercise in maintaining a healthy body. She jogged two miles three evenings a week, while the boys kept her company on their bicycles, and she regularly swam and played tennis at the club. She had no stomach to speak of, her breasts were high and firm, and unlike most women who had born children, she hadn't developed stretch marks on her hips. The tan she'd acquired on vacation showed up well against the dress, now that she noticed. Also *through* the dress, she realized with a grin.

"Gosh, mom, you look *pretty!*"

Todd delivered the compliment from her bedroom door, and Lacey smiled at him before smoothing a stray wisp of hair over her ear. She wore it cut short at the sides and back and only a little longer on top. It was a good basic razor cut, easy to care for, yet versatile.

"Honest Injun, pard?" she asked as she turned away from the mirror.

Todd nodded and came inside to climb up on her bed. He was still in his Smurf pajamas, his hair tousled, and when he rubbed the sleep from his eyes and yawned Lacey thought that there couldn't possibly be children anywhere as beautiful as hers.

"Well," she said as she sat beside him and finger-combed his silky hair, "personally, I think you're pretty neat, too, kiddo. Where's Scotty—still in bed?"

"Uh-huh. He's a sleepyhead this morning. Are you going to work early today?"

"Mm-hmm, a little bit. I have to show some people

a house at seven-thirty. They both work, and that's the only time they could make it. Come on, help me decide what shoes to wear, then we'll pull ol' lazy-bones out of bed and have breakfast together."

By the time they'd finished eating, Mrs. Moore had arrived. Lacey went directly to the house she was showing, and didn't get to the office until almost nine. As she came through the door Ellen and Vi, huddled at Ellen's desk, both looked up, guilt written all over their faces. *They're talking about me!* Lacey thought, surprised. She asked casually, "Any calls?" as she headed for her own office. She halted halfway to the door when the two older women exchanged looks, and Vi actually blushed.

"Well?" Lacey said impatiently. "Were there any calls for me?"

"Just one," Ellen answered. "Neil Hartmann called."

Lacey felt hot color climbing her neck, but forced her voice to remain brisk and businesslike. "And? Did he leave a message?"

"Not exactly," Ellen murmured. She shot another look at Vi, then explained. "First he asked if his wife was in—"

"He *what*?"

"And when I stopped stammering like a halfwit and said no, he asked what time you usually have lunch," Ellen finished. She sounded amused.

"I don't believe it!" Lacey breathed furiously. "The nerve, the sheer *gall*! I suppose you told him I go to lunch at twelve-thirty?"

"I'm afraid so," Ellen admitted, finally giving in to

the urge to smile. "He's a hard man to say no to. Is it true, Lacey? Is that gorgeous hunk really your husband?"

Lacey sighed in resignation. There was no use denying it. "Technically, yes. We're still legally married, but we've been separated for almost eight years."

Ellen looked at her for a minute, then said carefully, as if she wanted to be sure she had it straight: "Almost eight years. And the twins are seven, right?"

As Lacey stared back at the other woman, her face stiffened. "Yes," she whispered. "He doesn't know about them yet. Ellen, Vi . . . ." She appealed to them in turn with her eyes. This possibility hadn't even occurred to her that Neil might learn about the boys from somebody else.

"Don't worry, Lacey," Vi said with a kind smile. "He won't find out from us. Right, El?"

"Right!"

As the two women calmly went back to work, Lacey felt a warm rush of affection toward them both for their loyalty and understanding.

Both Ellen and Vi had worked for Jessie Meinert when Lacey first arrived here, a frightened twenty-two-year-old with no job prospects, no experience and two young sons to support. And, like Jessie, they had taken her under their wings from the very beginning.

As she sat at her desk, in what was now her office, she remembered those days from the vantage point of six years' distance.

She and the boys had left St. Louis virtually destitute, the remains of their last welfare check—about seventy-five dollars, all that remained of their cash reserves. They had nowhere to live, knew not a soul to turn to. She'd been utterly terrified and more alone than she could ever remember feeling in her life. There was no one anywhere who cared about her and her babies, no one to worry about them or even wonder if they were well and happy.

She had no friends to speak of, no contact with other young mothers her age, no basis on which to judge the way she lived. Her waking and sleeping thoughts, her very existence, had revolved around the twins: how to care for them, nurture them, provide the security they needed when she herself was so desperately insecure.

And then she met Jessie Meinert, and her whole life changed.

They had taken the bus from St. Louis, because that had been the cheapest form of transportation, and during the trip an elderly lady with kind brown eyes and a weathered face had offered to take charge of Todd while Lacey changed Scott's diaper. They introduced themselves, and then out of the blue, Jessie mentioned that she had an opening for a clerical worker in her real-estate office and asked if Lacey might be interested in having the job.

Lacey had been thunderstruck. To be offered a *job*, a means of supporting herself and her children, by practically the first person she met had seemed too good to be true. Honesty compelled her to confess that she knew next to nothing about real estate, but Jessie only shook her white head with a smile and replied that she looked like a fast learner.

She had been, and not just about the real estate business. During those first months she'd discovered the extent to which she'd been underestimating her own worth as a capable, competent human being. Neil had done such a hatchet job on her self-esteem that last night that it had been shattered almost beyond repair. But in three months Jessie Meinert had managed to instill in her a sense of self-worth that made everything else possible and remained with her.

Jessie had correctly sized her up that day on the bus, quickly and accurately reading her as a woman who'd had more than her fair share of trouble and pain, but recognizing her inner resources that would turn life's disappointments into personal triumphs.

In the beginning, Jessie had far more confidence in Lacey than Lacey had in herself. At first, she was almost afraid to believe that the days of struggle and hardship were over. It was difficult to adjust to the fact that she no longer had to squeeze every dollar until it squealed, to stretch every package of baloney to make it last until the next welfare check arrived in the mail. She never scrimped where the boys were concerned, but when it came to herself she was so tightfisted that Jessie finally had to take her in hand.

She *deserved* new clothes and an occasional meal out, Jessie told her sternly. She was working and working hard, paying her own way, and she'd earned the right to pamper herself a little, now and then. This job was *not* going to disappear overnight, the old woman told her, zeroing in on her innermost fears; and then to prove it, she'd enrolled Lacey in night school—paying the tuition herself—so that she'd have a realtor's license and the security that went with it.

Generous, was Jessie, and wise and deeply compassionate. She had been the only person to whom Lacey ever confided the story of her marriage, including that painful, humiliating last night. Not even Ellen and Vi had been trusted with the whole story, much as she loved and respected them. All they knew was that she'd married young and that the marriage had failed. It was only natural that they'd be curious, after the bombshell Neil had dropped that morning; but she knew their curiosity would be held in check until *she* decided to satisfy it, and for that she was deeply grateful.

With a sigh, she pulled herself out of the past and forced her thoughts to the work covering her desk. Twelve-thirty arrived without her being aware of it, and she might have worked right through lunch if Neil hadn't strolled into her office, carrying a bouquet of wild flowers.

Ellen's right, Lacey thought as she leaned back in her chair to look up at him: *he* is *a gorgeous hunk*. Today he was wearing a soft V-necked sweater of burnt orange, almost the same shade as his eyes in certain light, and deeper rust-colored slacks.

"For me?" she asked with false sweetness as she eyed the flowers.

"For you. To make up for yesterday," Neil answered with a crooked grin. "I *was* crude. Forgive?"

Lacey gave a noncommittal shrug and got up to fetch a water glass from the bathroom to put the flowers in.

"I remembered you like daisies and those blue things," he said as she carried the glass back to her desk without speaking. He slid a hip onto one desk corner and leaned close, tilting his head to one side to look into her face with an engaging grin. "I picked them all by myself. Aren't you impressed?"

Lacey took a step away from him and faced him squarely. "Just what do you mean by calling here and asking for your wife?"

Her tone was coldly condemning, her anger all the more cutting for being controlled. She saw the smile wiped from his face and his features set into a hard mask.

"That's what you are, Lacey. You might be ashamed to admit it, but I'm not. Sooner or later people are going to put two and two together, anyway. Especially when they start seeing us out together," he added.

For the moment Lacey ignored the challenge in those last words. She concentrated on controlling her temper and keeping her voice as level and emotionless as possible.

"You have got to be the most selfish man I've ever known," she said quietly. "The day you showed up here I told you I'd made a new life for myself, Neil. I don't just live and work in this town—I have friends here, people whose good opinion I value, who know nothing about my marriage except that I was very young and it didn't work out. I *belong*, Neil, in a way I never have before. And now you show up out of the blue determined to undermine the trust and respect it's taken me six years to earn. How do you think I felt when I came in this morning and found Vi and Ellen sniggering about that arrogant phone call of yours? I'll tell you how I felt—humiliated and then furious! How *dare* you! What gives you the right to bulldoze over other people's feelings that way? I won't stand for it, do you hear!"

Her battle for control was lost sometime during the last few sentences, and now she was trembling with rage, angry tears threatening to spill over as she glared at him. Neil seemed to have turned to stone. Only his eyes showed that he was at all affected by her tirade. They glittered with a strange light as they took in her agitated breathing and the tears shimmering in her hazel eyes.

"I apologize," he said quietly after a lengthy silence. "I swear, Lacey, I didn't intend to embarrass you." He sighed and stuck his hands into his pockets. "You're right, I am selfish. I guess I figured that if word got around that we're married, maybe some of those jocks you seem to collect might start to make themselves scarce," he admitted, a self-mocking smile tilting his mouth at one corner.

When Lacey just stared at him in angry disbelief, the smile spread. "Don't faint," he mocked with wry amusement. "I have occasionally been known to admit I'm wrong. Tell you what, from now on I won't refer to you as my wife to anybody. I'll leave it to you to tell the people you want to know. How's that?"

"Do you mean that?" she asked warily.

Neil lifted his right hand, three fingers extended stiffly. "Scout's honor. Now can we please call a truce, at least long enough to have lunch? I'm starved."

It would have been petty and childish to refuse, especially after he'd apologized so graciously. As he escorted her to his truck Lacey asked where they were going, and Neil flashed an almost boyish grin.

"It's a surprise."

He took her out to the farm he'd just bought, and after handing her down from the cab he removed a picnic basket and blanket from behind the seat.

"First I'd like you to go through the house with me, give me some ideas about what needs to be done inside," he said casually as he took her elbow to assist her across the overgrown lawn.

Lacey glanced at him suspiciously from under her lashes. If he thought there was any chance he was going to get her out here to live with him, he could darned well think again! She had her own house, convenient to the boys' school and her office. If this was part of his plan to convince her to take up married life again, it was doomed to failure from the start.

But despite her suspicions, Neil kept the conversation impersonal as they wandered through the big old farmhouse. He asked about closet space, whether she thought he should add one bathroom or two, what kind of insulation she'd recommend and remarked that he'd have to see about upgrading the electric service. Lacey was both surprised and relieved that he didn't drag her into the kitchen and demand to know how she'd remodel it if it was hers. By the time they went back outside she felt much more relaxed.

Neil spread the blanket under a huge old maple tree and unpacked the basket himself. There was cold chicken, a container of marinated raw vegetables, French bread, cheese and a chilled bottle of white wine. Lacey was flattered that he'd remembered what foods she liked; even the wine was one they'd shared before.

When the meal was finished she helped pack the things away, and then Neil settled himself against the trunk of the tree and drew her back against his chest, his arms around her in a loose embrace. Lulled into a relaxed contentment by the wine and his casual attitude, Lacey settled against him. She shifted a little to find a more comfortable position, then had to reach down and tug her skirt over her knees. The weather had been so warm lately, and her legs were so darkly tanned that she'd given up wearing panty hose for the summer.

"Did you have to do that?" Neil complained lazily, and she smiled as she let her head find a resting place on his shoulder.

"You were really serious about this courting business, weren't you?" she murmured in amusement.

"Absolutely. How do you like it so far?"

"It's a little soon to tell," Lacey hedged. Actually, she liked it very much but was reluctant to admit it just yet.

He slowly twined their fingers together in her lap, and his breath stirred the hair at her temple as he sighed.

"Give it a chance. I'll grow on you. Tell me about this new life you've made. For starters, how did you come to own a business called Meinert Realty and Insurance?"

Lacey smiled again at the humor in his voice. "It's named for Jessie Meinert, the previous owner. When I first came here she gave me a job, then sent me to school for my realtor's license. She was a spinster with no family, and when she died she left the business to me."

"She must have thought a lot of you," Neil commented quietly.

"I thought a lot of her, too. She was almost like a mother to me, and—" Lacey caught herself up short. She'd been about to say, "and a grandmother to the boys." Recovering quickly, she finished, "And we worked well together."

"You said you'd been here for six years. Where were you before that?"

"St. Louis," she replied tersely. St. Louis held bad memories, and she tried not even to think about the year and a half she'd spent there. She hoped Neil wouldn't question her about it.

"St. Louis!" he exclaimed in surprise. "Why the hell did you go there? We didn't know a soul in St. Louis."

"Exactly." Though Lacey tried, she couldn't quite keep the bitterness out of her voice. She knew he'd heard it when his arms tightened around her.

"I see," Neil murmured, then sighed again. "No wonder I couldn't find you."

"So you did try," Lacey said in a low, husky voice. There was a dull ache in her throat. He *had* come after her, then, and all her fears hadn't been groundless. When Neil released her hands to turn her roughly toward him she closed her eyes, not wanting him to see the power he still had to hurt her.

"Of course I tried!" he said harshly. "I nearly went out of my mind with worry! I looked everywhere—I even went to the hospital emergency rooms and the county morgue!" His voice quavered on the last word and Lacey's eyes flew open, her breath catching at the anguish she saw on his face.

"Neil!" she whispered tremulously. "You were telling the truth, weren't you? Last week, when you said you came back home that night ready to apologize?"

"I said I was ready to go down on my knees," he corrected grimly. "And yes, it was the truth. I'd do it now, if I thought it would help. Would it, Lacey? Could you forgive me if I begged?"

She could only shake her head dazedly, overwhelmed by an avalanche of conflicting emotions. "Oh, Neil," she said with a catch in her voice. "I don't know what to say. Forgive you? Maybe I could—I'm not sure. I thought I'd put that night behind me, and then you showed up and brought it all back as if it happened yesterday. I just don't know," she repeated softly, almost to herself.

Seeing the distress in her troubled eyes, Neil lifted a hand to tenderly stroke her cheek. His touch was strangely comforting, soothing.

"I'm so mixed up," Lacey whispered. "I don't even know what I feel right now."

"Then let me tell you what I feel," Neil offered. He pulled her head against his chest and bent to lay his cheek on her hair.

"I love you, Lacey." His deep, resonant voice throbbed with intensity. "I love you now, I loved you ten years ago, and I'll love you just as much on my dying day. I need you and want you, but most of all I love you. I realize you probably can't believe that, but I'll keep on telling you until I *make* you believe. My life's been like a desert the past eight years. I know I don't deserve it, but I want another chance. I want it desperately. Now that I've found you, I don't think I could survive losing you again." At the end his voice became unsteady, and he crushed her to him, as if he was afraid she might disappear again if he didn't hold on tight.

Lacey's eyes were closed, but she heard his words and felt the warmth of his body, the hard strength of his arms. Still she felt she must be dreaming. This couldn't be Neil, claiming that he loved her, had always loved her! Hot tears leaked from under her lashes and ran unchecked down her cheeks.

For eight years she'd despised and feared him, and all that time he had existed in his own private hell of guilt and loneliness. But it was too late to make amends and start over, she thought miserably. There was too much of a gulf between them for things to ever be the same. She wasn't a twenty-year-old girl anymore, she was a grown woman, a mother. . . .

She *had* to tell him now, she saw that clearly. She lifted her head from his shoulder, praying for the words to do it without burdening him with still more guilt. But before she could, Neil saw her tears.

"No! Oh, Lacey, no!" he groaned, and then he was kissing her, first her damp cheeks, then her eyes and finally her mouth. His lips were firm but gentle, soothing, healing, while his hands tenderly framed her face. Rational thought deserted her. She forgot everything but how incredibly gentle he could be. It had always surprised her, the way his lovemaking would shift without warning from wild, totally abandoned passion to an almost delicate gentleness and back again, with a swiftness that stole the breath from her body.

Lacey was unconsciously waiting, anticipating the moment when his mouth would harden in possession and his hands would drop down her body, seeking and finding all the pleasure points he knew so well. But she waited in vain; this time the gentleness continued, until at last the tension had drained out of her and she lay limply in his arms.

"Better?" he asked softly, and Lacey nodded as she nestled against his chest. Neil's lips touched the slightly upturned tip of her nose. "Right now you don't look a day older than the first time I saw you. You were wearing some short frilly white thing that showed off those nonstop legs, and you looked like a lamb who'd wandered into the middle of a pack of wolves. I took one look and knew my bachelor days were numbered. All that innocence was just irresistible."

"You were a randy old lecher," Lacey teased with a smile.

Neil smiled back, a tender, somewhat indulgent smile totally unlike his usual sardonic humor.

"I still am," he murmured, then bent to kiss her softly on the mouth. "As soon as I saw you I knew I had to have you, and once I had you I wanted to lock you up, keep you all to myself. I was scared to death some young buck would come along and take you away from me."

Lacey digested that in silence. He was only half joking, she sensed, and she suddenly saw in a new light the days and nights she'd spent alone while he was busy with business meetings. He'd discouraged her friendships with people her own age, claiming she was a married woman now, and her responsibility was to her husband. At the time she'd considered his attitude arrogant and selfish, but might he really have been insecure, afraid he couldn't compete with the younger men in the crowd she ran with before he came along?

"For a while I thought you were ashamed of me," Lacey said quietly, watching his face. "I started to think you'd only married me for my body, that you didn't want me around your friends, the people you worked with, because you were afraid I'd make some terrible faux pas and embarrass you in front of them."

Neil shook his head in denial. "Ashamed of you?" he repeated roughly. "God, I felt like the luckiest man in the world. You'd married me—*me*—when you could have had your pick of a dozen young studs. But I'm seventeen years older than you, Lacey, and I've never been able to let my hair down and relax with other people. I lived in mortal fear that someday you'd look at me and see this dull, aging stuffed shirt and realize what a mistake you'd made."

Lacey marveled at the confession. She'd never even

guessed that so much doubt and uncertainty was concealed behind the cool, self-assured exterior. If she'd only known!

"You were the only stud I ever wanted." Though she smiled, the statement was delivered without a trace of humor. "I married you because I *had* to, Neil, because after I met you my life wouldn't have been complete without you. I thought you knew that. All I ever wanted was for you to love me even half as much as I loved you, and to let me share your life, as an equal. You made me feel inferior, like some brainless child you only tolerated during the day because of what I could give you at night."

Neil closed his eyes and rested his forehead against hers. "I wish to God we'd talked like this before," he said with feeling. "I could see you weren't happy, but I thought it was because I wasn't what you'd expected, that you were already disappointed with marriage, with me. I drove myself like a fiend to make more money, build more security, thinking that if I got far enough ahead I could retire early and be with you all the time, like I wanted. But it seemed the harder I worked, the further apart we grew."

He stopped and pulled back to look at her.

"That first year, I used to pray you'd get pregnant," he said, and Lacey's heart skipped a beat. This was the first time he'd ever mentioned wanting children, and a wild hope leaped in her breast. "I thought if I gave you a child, a part of me to love while I was trying to secure our future, it might keep us together until I could work things out. Now, of course, I'm glad we didn't have a baby, but at the time I was grasping at straws."

The hope turned to cold, thick dread in Lacey's throat. "But a baby might have helped," she said tentatively. "I always wanted to have your children, Neil, even in the beginning. I didn't think *you* wanted any."

"Oh, I did." He sighed heavily. "But for all the wrong reasons. Looking back, I can see what a mistake it would have been to start a family when our marriage was already so shaky. About the only thing I've had to be thankful for in the past eight years was that we *didn't* have a child."

Lacey didn't contradict him, didn't speak at all, in fact. She was afraid she wouldn't be able to hide how much his words had hurt, each one carrying the force of a physical blow. Neil must have mistaken her silence as thoughtful reflection, because he didn't question it or try to draw her out for several minutes. Finally he stirred and laid a light kiss on her forehead.

"Do you have to go back in this afternoon?"

"Yes," Lacey murmured, not quite meeting his eyes. "I've got a couple of appointments, and some claims to approve."

"Okay, then I guess we'd better hit the road." But he was obviously reluctant to end their time together, and on the way into town he remarked, rather sharply Lacey thought, "You need to increase your staff, hire more help than you've got now."

Lacey bit down on her resentment at his autocratic tone. "Usually I *have* more help. It's just that the two women who sell for me part-time happened to take their vacations at the same time this year, and Rick Baker—he's my full-time salesman—is away for six weeks at summer school. He's finishing up work on a B.B.A."

"Rick Baker—any relation to Gary Baker?"

"His son. You know Gary?" Lacey asked in surprise.

Neil shrugged. "We were in high school at the same time. What's he doing now?"

"He's a vice-president at Farmer's Bank and Trust."

Neil merely arched one brow in mild surprise. He accompanied Lacey into her office to complete the paperwork for the farm sale, then turned her desk calendar toward him and ran an idle finger down the list of appointments for that day.

" 'Seven-thirty, dinner, c.c.,' " he read aloud, then looked up and asked, "Chamber of Commerce dinner?"

"No. A directors' dinner meeting at the country club."

Neil didn't bother to hide his surprise. "You're a *director*?"

Lacey felt another stab of resentment. She knew what he was getting at: it was unusual for women to hold memberships in country clubs under their own names. Usually they only gained entrance through their husbands' or fathers' memberships.

"It just so happens that I was one of the original two hundred founding members," she told him coolly. "The club's only been in existence a little over three years, and we're mostly a young group of business and professional people. It gives us a place to entertain clients and customers, and we use it as much for business meetings as for social functions. Does that satisfy your curiosity?"

His forehead creased in a frown. "Why so defensive all of a sudden?"

Lacey shrugged uneasily. She couldn't tell him the real reason she'd been tense and on edge ever since they left the farm, not now, not until she'd had some time to think.

Neil sighed in impatience. "I wasn't putting you down, Lacey. Believe it or not, the more I find out about how much you've accomplished on your own, the more proud of you I am. It's just that it's a little hard to take it all in. Eight years ago you couldn't even balance a checkbook," he reminded her.

"That's a pompous chauvinistic remark, Neil, and I resent it," Lacey retorted. "How on earth would you know whether or not I could have balanced a checkbook. You didn't even trust me to carry one!"

"That's not true!" he denied, looking surprised.

"It *is* true! You gave me a walletful of plastic money so you could keep tabs on how much I spent and what I spent it on, but I couldn't be trusted to write checks, and I nearly forgot whose picture was on a dollar bill! I didn't even know how much it cost to run that ridiculous apartment. Four bedrooms and five baths, Neil, all for two people, plus a private sauna and a putting green on the roof you never had time to use! So much waste—it was obscene!"

"I thought you liked our home," he said quietly.

"It wasn't a home," Lacey told him in a tired voice.

"It was just a place to sit and wait for you to come back to when you were finished with your meetings and wanted a little sex."

His mouth thinned, and there was a hard glint in his eyes. "Is that all it was to you—sex?" he demanded tautly.

Lacey forced herself to meet his gaze and answered honestly. "Yes, Neil, that's all it was. I won't deny it was enjoyable, but I never felt it meant anything more to you than satisfying a physical need. That's why that last night was so horrible—you just confirmed what I'd thought all along, that I wasn't important to you in any other way, that I was just a convenient body, somebody to *use* when the urge struck."

The color faded from his face, leaving his features strained and white. When she'd finished, he abruptly got out of his chair and turned away, his hands shoved deep in his trouser pockets as he paced to the other side of the office. Lacey knew she had hurt him, but she felt no remorse. After what he'd said about children—saying they'd have been a mistake, and he was thankful they hadn't had any—she supposed a part of her had wanted to lash out at him in return, to wound him as he'd wounded her. Still, if she didn't feel remorse, neither did she feel any satisfaction as he turned back to her, and she saw the pinched look around his mouth and nose and the way his eyes were defensively hooded.

"It seems I've got a lot more to make up for than I thought," he said quietly. "Will you let me, Lacey? Will you at least let me try?"

The almost humble appeal in his voice was very nearly her undoing. Her shoulders sagged as she slowly shook her head. She felt mentally and emotionally exhausted, drained.

"Oh, Neil, what's the use? It's too late to start over, can't you see that? We're not the same people we were then. It just wouldn't work."

He came to face her across the desk, bracing his hands on it as he leaned down to look long and hard into her eyes.

"It's not too late," he denied harshly. "Not unless we want it to be, and I don't! I want you back, Lacey. Back in my life, where you belong." He stood back to take a deep breath and run a hand through his hair. "I've pushed you too hard, when I swore I'd give you some time to get used to the idea. All right," he said on a resigned sigh, "I'll back off a little. I won't come around for a while, or call you, but you have to promise to think about it, Lacey. I mean *really* think about it," he stressed. "I'm not talking about a trial run. I want a full commitment from you, because that's what I'm offering. I know we can make it work if we try, but we both have to be convinced it's what we want—a real marriage, a partnership that'll last the rest of our lives."

After he'd gone Lacey sat staring into space for nearly an hour. At first she'd been filled with relief when he promised not to come around or call for a while; it would give her much needed time. Not time to consider what Neil was asking of her—she didn't know if there would ever be enough time in her life to reach that decision. She needed this time to decide how to tell him about his sons. He had given her a reprieve, but she knew that was all it was. He intended to stay, to make his home here, taking the decision about *whether* to tell him out of her hands. If she didn't, sooner or later someone else would. And heaven only knew how he'd react if he found out about them from anyone else.

5

NEIL HAD ALWAYS BEEN a man of action, so Lacey wasn't really surprised when Gary Baker submitted his name for membership in the country club that very night. She did kick herself for unintentionally opening the door for him, though she had no doubt at all that Neil would have managed it on his own. Things would just have taken a little longer.

She listened with all the others while Gary sang the praises of Neil Hartmann, pointing out that he was not only a native son but also an enormously successful man whose experience and "savvy" could prove invaluable to the business community now that he'd decided to retire in his hometown. Leave it to Gary to see the practical benefits of a membership for Neil, Lacey thought with a touch of cynicism. Or, more likely, leave it to Neil to have stressed his business acumen when he approached Gary. After all, he'd been armed with the information *she* had provided about the club that very afternoon!

When Gary suddenly turned to her with a beaming smile, her hands clenched in her lap. *Here it comes*, she thought with grim resignation. Paul shifted in his seat beside her, then reached over under cover of the table and laid his hand on her fists. Lacey appreciated the gesture, but she kept her eyes on Gary Baker.

"Sorry if I've stepped on your toes, Lacey," he said cheerfully, and she gritted her teeth. "You see," he explained to the others, "by rights, Lacey should have presented Neil's name for membership. But though she was his first contact in town, I'm claiming that privilege because I've known him longer. Neil tells me he's bought the old Miller homestead. Right, Lacey?"

"That's right," she managed to murmur. He didn't know! Gary really didn't know! Neil had kept his word, after all. But following on the heels of a twinge of guilt came the realization that he had very adroitly put the ball smack in her court. The next move was hers, and Gary gave her the perfect opening.

"Well, as the first of us to do business with him, Lacey, don't you agree he'd be an asset to the club?" His smile was benevolent, even a little smug. Poor man, he thought he'd scored quite a coup in presenting Neil to the rest of them. It was almost a shame to burst his bubble.

"I'm not sure I'm the best person to give a reference for Neil Hartmann," Lacey murmured in a dry tone. Then she smiled almost apologetically. "You see, Gary, I'm his estranged wife."

An hour later she and Paul were having coffee in the dinette adjoining Lacey's kitchen. The twins were in bed, and Mrs. Moore had gone. With a grin Paul shook his head.

"I thought poor Gary was going to choke. I believe that is what's known as dropping a bombshell."

"You think it's amusing, do you?" Lacey asked. She wasn't smiling.

Paul shrugged and sipped his coffee. "The situation he put you in, no, that is not amusing. But you must admit that the looks on their faces ranged from comical to hilarious. You do realize that with the directors' recommendation, the membership committee is sure to accept him? Will it disturb you to come in frequent contact with him?"

Lacey stared down into her cup. "If Neil has his way, our contact will be more than just frequent," she said quietly. She felt Paul's eyes on her and reluctantly lifted her head to meet them. His expression was solemn, thoughtful.

"I see. And you . . . how do you feel? Do you want what he wants?"

"Oh, Paul, I don't know! I haven't even adjusted to the fact that he's actually here!" She rubbed her fingertips at the spot over the bridge of her nose where a headache was trying to take hold. "For myself, the answer is an unequivocal no. The last thing I want is to become involved with him again. But I have to think of the boys. Do I have the right to deny them a normal family life?"

"Yes," Paul murmured in agreement, "that is a problem. How did he react when you told him about them?"

"I haven't," Lacey admitted heavily.

"Lacey!"

"I know. I *know!*" She hesitated, not wanting to tell him everything. "It's a difficult situation, Paul. I just haven't been able to find the right way to do it."

"But you must, and soon!" he insisted. "After tonight, it is only a matter of time until someone mentions his sons to him."

"You're right," she admitted. "I'll have to tell him the first chance I get. The next time he comes by—"

"Don't wait for him to come by!" Paul sounded exasperated. "Call him yourself, or seek him out. Lacey, you have already put this off far too long!"

She was shaking her head wearily but adamantly. "No, I can't be the one to make the next move. If I went to him, he'd take it as a sign that I'd given in. It would be like waving a white flag."

"You make it sound like a war," Paul said skeptically.

She sighed. "In a way, it is. A war of wills. I lost the last one, but I have no intention of losing this one. No, I'll just have to wait for him to contact me again. Knowing Neil, I doubt if it'll be very long," she added dryly.

In fact, an entire week went by without a sign of Neil. Tidbits of information trickled in to her about him: he'd hired a plumbing contractor and a roofing contractor and practically bought out the town's two lumber companies. People who came into the office were full of news about the eccentric millionaire who'd bought the old Miller place out on Claypool Road and was throwing money away on it hand over fist, which told Lacey that word apparently hadn't spread that she and Neil were married. In a way she was glad, but it also made her uncomfortable to have to stand and listen politely to the latest gossip about him. What were these people going to think when they found out they'd been passing on rumors and bits of speculation to his *wife*? They'd be embarrassed, certainly. Enough to take their business elsewhere?

"Oh, what a tangled web we weave . . ." she told herself as she locked up the office on the Friday afternoon of the following week. In all fairness, if she was going to be angry or irritated, it had to be at herself. Neil was only keeping his word, after all; it was up to her to set the record straight about their relationship. But why hadn't he called or come by the office? Was he trying to wear her down by straining her nerves to the breaking point?

After supper she worked off some of her tension by running two miles. Instead of following her into the driveway when they returned home, the boys rode their bikes up the block to the Crawfords'. Danny Crawford was their age, and his brother Brian a year older. The four of them were nearly inseparable; if they weren't playing at the Crawfords', they were usually at Lacey's. She called after them to be home before dark, then raised the garage door to take out the lawn mower.

Forty-five minutes later she was hot and sweaty, red in the face and sporting several shallow but nasty-looking scratches from a pyracantha bush. Although the plant was supposed to train itself to climb the wall on the far side of the garage, it chose to grow straight out into the yard. Every time she tried to mow under it the long thorns flayed the mower, herself, or both.

"Damned menace," Lacey muttered as she shut off

the mower. "That's the last time you lie in wait for me. I should have done this months ago."

She pushed the mower back into the garage, then came out again carrying a handsaw. She was in the middle of amputating the last branch when Neil's truck pulled into the drive. She didn't even hear the quiet, powerful engine and only straightened in surprise when he exclaimed, "What do you think you're doing!"

Lacey's head snapped up and she stared at him with her mouth open. It hadn't even occurred to her that he might come to the house.

"You look like you just fought the battle of Armageddon," he drawled as he frowned at her, hands on his hips. "And lost."

"There's the culprit," she said, indicating the stack of branches at her feet. "Percy Pyracantha. But he's slashed his last victim, the vicious little carnivore."

Neil's bushy eyebrows rose in amused surprise. "Percy Pyracantha?" he repeated soberly.

Lacey nodded and barely managed to keep her own mouth from curving into a smile. Of course he thought it was funny for a grown woman to be naming shrubs and bushes. Actually, it was the boys' doing; they named everything, even the spiders they occasionally found in the laundry room.

"Looks like you could use some first aid," he remarked as he eyed her bare limbs, and for the first time Lacey became aware of how she must look.

She was still wearing her running clothes: bright green shorts and a tank top, jogging shoes with a yellow stretch terry sweatband around her head. The picture of poise and sophistication, she thought wryly. But come to think of it, he wasn't exactly dressed to kill, either. He had on a plain blue chambray work shirt, sneakers and jeans—*jeans!* Since when had Neil owned a pair of jeans? Or sneakers, either, for that matter? One heavy black brow quirked when he noticed the way she was staring at him, and he spread his arms and did a slow turn in the middle of the sidewalk.

"Like it? It's the latest in menswear from Levi Strauss."

"Mucho macho," Lacey approved soberly, and he grinned.

"Aren't you going to invite me in? I could kiss your scratches all better."

"I think I can manage," she answered. "But I will ask you in. There's something I need to talk to you about."

She offered coffee or lemonade, and he surprised her by asking for the lemonade. He wandered around the kitchen while she got ice from the freezer and poured them each a tall glass.

"Nice house," he remarked as he peered around the corner of the dinette, where the floor plan divided into upper and lower levels. "Bedrooms upstairs and rumpus room down, right?"

"We call it the family room," Lacey corrected absently. She found the box of antiseptic pads in a cabinet and started cleaning the scratches on her arms and legs. There was one on her left elbow deeper than the rest, and she winced slightly as the antiseptic stung. Neil was suddenly at her side, his long fingers cool on her skin as they curved around her arm.

"Here, let me." He took a fresh pad from the box and very gently cleaned the scratch. Lacey made herself stand absolutely still, though her instinctive urge was to pull out of his grasp and move away.

She had to keep her wits about her, she told herself sternly. It was foolish and weak-minded to let his touch, his very nearness, affect her like this. She thought she caught a whiff of turpentine. Had he been painting? Odd, she somehow couldn't picture Neil with a paintbrush in his hand. A telephone, a brandy snifter, one of his specially blended cigars—she could imagine those lean, strong fingers holding many different things, but not a brush dripping wet paint. Her eyes lifted and then widened in astonishment.

"You've got blue paint in your hair!"

Neil's lips twitched at the disbelief in her voice, then he bent to plant a light kiss on her elbow.

"There, all better. You like that shade of blue, don't you? At least you used to."

"Yes. I mean, I still do, but—"

"Good. I'm glad I haven't wasted a whole afternoon and two gallons of paint. Don't ask, it's a surprise," he said as he perched on a stool at the breakfast bar and took a long thirsty drink of his lemonade. "Mmm, that hit the spot. What was it you wanted to talk to me about?"

Lacey felt a mixture of nervousness and exasperation. Neil never gave anything away, and nothing got to him unless he let it. What would it take to shatter that iron control? She was tempted to simply blurt out that he had two seven-year-old sons and see if that would do it, but before she could act, Neil muttered something and slid off the stool, striding angrily across the room.

"Good Lord, this one must be a midget," he said in disgust as he bent to pick up an object on one of the chair seats.

He held it up, and Lacey nearly burst out laughing. It was one of Todd's—or maybe Scott's—shin guards.

"Do all your lovers leave their equipment lying around the house?" he grated as he flung the slim piece of curved plastic onto the table. "And are they *all* dwarfs?"

Lacey conquered the hysterical urge to giggle. "No, to both questions. As a matter of fact, that happens to belong to—"

"*Mom!*"

The sound of the front door slamming punctuated the childishly high-pitched call. Lacey halted with her mouth still open. Neil's face went very still, and then a look of contempt came into his startled eyes.

"My God, Lacey!" His voice was low and harsh, an accusation. No, worse, a condemnation.

"Mom! You in the house?"

"In the kitchen," she called back. She folded her arms as she held Neil's eyes.

"Me and Todd want to know—"

"Todd and I," Lacey corrected automatically as Scott strolled through the kitchen door. She watched Neil's face closely as he got his first look at the boy.

She estimated it took about three seconds for the realization to clobber him over the head.

"Todd and I want to know can we sleep outside in the tent tonight, and can Danny and Brian come, too? Their mom says okay if you do. Hello." The last word was directed with a dimpled grin at Neil.

Neil swallowed hard, as if there was something large lodged in his throat. His face had drained of all color. "Hello," he responded in a hoarse whisper.

"Well, can we, mom?"

The front door slammed again, and Lacey drew a deep breath.

"Scott, did you ask her? What did she say?"

Running feet sounded across the tiled entry and were muffled by the dinette carpet before Todd skidded to a halt beside his brother just inside the kitchen.

"Mom? Can we? *Please?* It's not gonna rain. We listened to the radio already, and Mrs. Crawford said it's okay with her if it is with you."

Breathless and wide-eyed with anticipation, Todd gazed up at his mother. He didn't notice the stranger standing rigid with shock on the other side of the table until Scott nudged him in the ribs and jerked his head in that direction.

"Oh, hi," Todd said sheepishly, then grinned. His grin was identical to Scott's, right down to the dimples. One of Neil's hands groped for the back of a chair. His pallor and the glazed look in his eyes worried Lacey. She'd known it would be a shock, but he actually looked as if he might pass out.

"All right," she said hastily, diverting the boys' attention. "Go tell Danny and Brian it's okay, and then the four of you can get the tent out of the garage."

They ran out with whoops of glee, and she turned to Neil in concern. "Are you all right?"

He nodded jerkily and drew a deep, ragged-sounding breath, then crossed to the bar. His back was to Lacey, but she saw him reach up toward his shirt pocket. He took something out of it—she thought it was a flat pillbox—and then his hand went to his mouth before he took a couple of quick gulps of the lemonade.

"Neil? Are you sure you're all right?"

His hand moved again, to replace the pillbox or whatever, she supposed, before he turned toward her. He was still pale, but his eyes burned with accusing anger.

"No, I'm not all right!" he grated. "You didn't tell me! Good Lord, Lacey, you've had over two weeks, and you deliberately kept it from me. How could you?" He broke off to rake an unsteady hand through his hair. "You wouldn't have told me, would you? You'd have let me find out from some damned stranger on the street. Do you really hate me that much?"

"*No!* Neil, I—" She took a step toward him, then stopped, spreading her hands helplessly. "I'm sorry. I know it was wrong not to tell you about the boys, but try to understand. At first, I didn't know you intended to stay here permanently. I thought you'd be going back to Denver, and it didn't seem fair to disrupt all our lives for the sake of a few days once or twice a year, when you could spare the time to fit in a visit."

Neil heard her out in a grim, tight-lipped silence, his hands gripping the edge of the bar at his back so hard his knuckles showed white.

"All right," he said quietly. "I'll accept that—you were thinking of them. But you've known I intended to stay since last Wednesday, and why. Out at the farm, when we talked...I thought I was getting through to you, Lacey. Do you have any idea how hard it was for me to open up to you like that? Didn't it mean anything that I bared my soul, that I all but begged?" he asked savagely.

"Yes," Lacey whispered tearfully. "I do know, and it did mean something."

"Then *why*? Why didn't you tell me about my sons?" he demanded bitterly. "It would have been the perfect time."

"I started to," she said in a muffled voice. "I *wanted* to, but then you said...." Her voice faltered, and she took a gulping breath in a futile attempt to steady it. "You said that you'd decided having children would have been a mistake, and that you were thankful we hadn't had a child." The last words were wrenched out in a painful spasm as she furiously blinked back tears.

Neil closed his eyes and, if possible, paled even more. "Oh, no," he said in a strangled voice. He swallowed again, convulsively, and then both his eyes and his arms were open as he came to her.

"Don't cry, baby," he said roughly. "It's all right, don't cry."

"I'm sorry," Lacey blubbered into his shirt as she clung to him. "I'm sorry I didn't tell you. I meant to,

Neil, I really did. I've been worried sick somebody else would before I could find a way."

"Shh, shh. It's all right, I understand," he soothed. His hands gently stroked her back and he bent to lay soft kisses on her eyelids. "I was thinking of myself when I said those things last week," he confessed in a rough voice. "Of what it was like to grow up knowing I didn't belong anywhere, to anybody. I only meant I wouldn't want a child of mine—*any* child— to grow up like that."

"I should have realized," Lacey murmured. She sniffled and wiped at her cheeks, then leaned back against his arms to look into his face. "But now that you've seen them, what do you think of your sons?" she asked huskily. Her eyes were dark, her mouth quivering and vulnerable.

Neil shook his head, for a moment too moved to answer. "My sons," he repeated, a note of wonder in his voice, and then he caught her to him, holding her tight. "They're beautiful," he said roughly. "Damned near perfect. How did we make two kids like that?"

Lacey's laugh was shaky with nervous relief. "The usual way," she said lightly. Then her breath seemed to catch in her throat, and Neil drew back a little to look at her.

"What is it?" he asked with a frown.

Lacey pulled out of his embrace and turned her back on him. When she answered, her voice was low and throaty.

"Todd and Scott were conceived that last night," she said simply. "Those two beautiful, nearly perfect children are the result of that night, Neil."

He didn't speak, and she didn't dare turn toward him. She hugged her arms tight across her middle, as if the pain in her heart had spread and needed containing. After a few seconds that seemed like centuries Neil slipped his arms around her from behind. She could feel the erratic beat of his heart behind his chest wall, and knew he was reliving that night, too.

"There isn't anything I can say that would be enough," he murmured above her head.

Lacey agreed. "No. Not now."

"Does that mean it's too late?"

She shook her head listlessly. "I don't know, Neil," she replied. "At a guess, I'd have to say yes, it's probably too late. For us, at least."

"I still love you, Lacey," he said softly. "Doesn't that count for anything? I love you, and I want to be with you—with all of you."

She gave a bitter little laugh. "Love? We seem to have different ideas about what it means, Neil. You claim you loved me eight years ago, but you sure had a strange way of showing it."

"Stop it!"

His hands suddenly shot out to seize her shoulders, his fingers digging into her flesh until she gasped in pain. His face was a taut white mask. "You think you're the only one who's had to live with that night, Lacey? You think I haven't suffered, too?"

"Suffered?" she responded scornfully. "Oh yes, I can just imagine the suffering and torment you went through, Neil, living in your luxurious penthouse apartment, driving to work in a thirty-thousand-dollar car, going to bed at night between silk sheets.

You want to know about suffering? Suffering is having to resort to welfare checks to keep your children fed and clothed—"

She broke off suddenly, her voice quavering as the fear, shame and indignity of that time returned in a wave of fury.

"It was degrading and dehumanizing, and I hated it. I *hated* it!" she choked, her fists clenching in impotent rage.

Neil spun away, but not before she saw the ravaged look in his eyes.

"I didn't know. How could I have known?"

Lacey had her wish. His control had finally snapped, but instead of satisfaction all she felt was a faintly nauseating remorse for having brought him to this. She closed her eyes and took a few deep breaths to bring herself under control again.

"You couldn't," she admitted in a flat, emotionless voice. "Anymore than I could have known what you were going through. I'm sorry, Neil. I didn't mean to...bring all that up," she said inadequately. "I just...that first year and a half was so bad, I try not to even think about it. But I got through it—all three of us did, and if there are scars they're all mine, and they're all pretty much healed. The boys were too young to know or remember any of it."

She hesitated, then took the two steps necessary to bring her within touching distance. Her hand faltered in midair for a moment before it came to rest on his shoulder. There had been enough hurting, on both sides. It was time to really put the past behind them, if only for the sake of the boys' future.

"They're terrific kids, Neil," she said softly. "But they're reaching the age where they need a man around to serve as a role model. They need their father," she murmured. "I'd like to share them with you. It's not too late for that, at least."

Neil turned slowly. His features were composed, but there was an unmistakable sheen of moisture in his eyes. As Lacey's hand dropped, he caught and held it tight.

"I don't know a damned thing about being a father," he said harshly. "I'm forty-five years old, and I haven't had anything to do with kids since *I* was one. This may be the biggest mistake you've ever made."

He was watching her intently, and Lacey shook her head with the suggestion of a smile. "Somehow I don't think so."

"What if they hate me?"

"They won't," she said confidently. "In the first place, I don't think it's in them to hate. They haven't learned how to, yet. And I've never criticized you to them, tried to turn them against you. I wouldn't do that, Neil."

The slight relaxing of his body told her she'd answered his unspoken question as he pulled her into his arms. He held her tight, but there was no passion in the embrace, only relief and gratitude. Lacey slipped her arms around his chest, once more surprised by the faint odor of turpentine as her cheek lay against his shirt. She could just make out a slight bulge in the pocket, and wanted to ask him about it, but this didn't seem to be the time.

"Thank you." His deep, rough voice rumbled beneath Lacey's ear, and she gave him a brief squeeze of acknowledgment. His sigh lifted her head slightly as his chest rose and fell.

"For what it's worth, Lacey, I'll try to be as good a father to them as you've been a mother. God only knows whether or not I'll succeed, but I'll give it everything I've got."

"I know you will," she murmured, and she suddenly believed it. A massive weight seemed to lift from her shoulders, and she raised her head to smile at him softly. Neil smiled back, and her breath caught at the warmth in his eyes.

"The thing is...where do I start?" he asked with a crook of one shaggy brow.

Lacey started to reply that he'd just have to take things as they came, like every other parent, and then a commotion outside the patio door at the end of the dinette caught her attention. Todd, Scott and the Crawford boys were struggling valiantly with the four-man tent, each one apparently trying to direct the others. Her smile widened.

"Well... do you know how to pitch a tent?" she asked with a grin.

6

As LACEY AND NEIL stepped onto the patio they made an unspoken agreement not to reveal his identity to the twins that night. They both wanted to wait until the four of them could be alone.

Once Neil had been recruited by the boys, Lacey stood back and watched, not offering help or advice with the tent pitching until Neil finally looked up at her in exasperation and muttered, "For pity's sake, woman, don't just stand there with your teeth in your mouth! Can't you see we need a hand?"

All four children gurgled with enjoyment, and when Lacey smiled and obliged by giving them all a round of applause their giggles turned to peals of laughter, while Neil rolled his eyes and groaned. He stood up in one lithe movement, grabbed her by a wrist and dragged her into the tent. After they helped the children spread their sleeping bags inside, Lacey fetched two flashlights and a transistor radio from the house.

"Eight to one the batteries will all be dead in the morning," she said as she and Neil returned to the kitchen. "How about a cup of coffee?"

"Thanks," he accepted easily.

He parked himself on one of the cane-and-leather

bar stools and watched while she prepared two cups. Lacey hadn't been at all nervous or self-conscious while they were with the children, but now suddenly she was both. Neil thanked her again when she brought him his coffee, then hooked a toe under the tubular chrome footrest of the stool next to his and pulled it away from the bar for her to sit on. It was too obvious a gesture to ignore.

"You were right," he said quietly when she was seated beside him. "They are terrific kids."

Lacey smiled as she clasped both hands around her cup. "Of course we could be just a little bit biased."

His solemn expression softened, and he smiled back. "Maybe just a little," he agreed, then reached over as she set her cup down and took her hand in a light clasp. "But even allowing for parental pride, I'd have to say those are two dynamite kids. And not as identical as I thought at first, either. Scott seems to be more like you—easygoing, slow to rile. But Todd's got my temperament. Or maybe I should say my temper," he amended wryly. "If there'd been a tree handy, I think he might have wrapped that stake around it."

Lacey stared at him in amazement. Most people who'd known the twins for years still couldn't tell one from the other, yet after less than an hour in their company Neil had accurately identified the basic differences in their personalities.

She told him how impressed she was, adding with a trace of awe, "Even their pediatrician mixes them up now and then."

Neil shrugged off the idea that there was anything

unusual about his perception. "Blood calls to blood,"
he said in explanation. Then his gaze seemed to
sharpen. "You mentioned their pediatrician. They're
healthy, aren't they? I mean, no physical problems?"

"Oh no," Lacey assured him quickly. "They seem
to have inherited your constitution," she added with
a smile. "They hardly ever even have colds. I have to
admit to being a little overprotective, though. I can
handle the scraped knees and stubbed toes all right,
but at the first sign of a cough or fever I head straight
for the doctor's office. Serious illness, even the
thought of it, throws me into a panic," she admitted
with an involuntary little shiver.

Neil frowned as he turned his hand to link their fingers. "I don't remember you being frightened of sick-
ness." His voice was low, almost guarded.

"You'd remember, if you'd ever been sick," Lacey
said grimly. "I go to pieces whenever anyone I care
about is seriously ill. I think it started when one of
my friends in school died of leukemia. She was like a
sister to me, and she was very ill for a long time. And
then something happened when the boys were babies
that made it worse."

Neil turned sideways on the stool. "Tell me."
When he saw her reluctance he reached up to turn her
face toward him, his fingers under her chin, forcing
her to meet his eyes.

"Come on, Lacey," he insisted softly. "I have a
right to know. And I'm a big boy—I can take it," he
added in a mocking drawl.

She kept her eyes lowered, acutely conscious of the
warm pressure of his fingers on her skin. "When they

were eight months old, I left them with a neighbor one afternoon to apply for a job at a discount store that was opening in our area. It was winter, and there was already a long line of people with the same idea outside the store. I caught a cold. A couple of days later it developed into pneumonia, and I had to go into the hospital. The county put the boys in a foster home until I was strong enough to take care of them again."

She lifted her eyes then, and the look on Neil's face cut her to the quick. She reached up to take his hand.

"They couldn't have done anything else. I had no family or close friends the boys could have stayed with, and the foster couple were very nice—elderly, and kind-hearted. It was just knowing they *could* be taken from me, simply because I got sick. Not being able to see them, hold them, was torture, and I couldn't help worrying that something would happen because I wasn't there to take care of them myself.

"Anyway," she shrugged, attempting to ease the tension she could feel in Neil's hands, "now you know what's behind my terror of illness. I *know* it's neurotic, but I can't help it. I don't take any chances. We eat well-balanced meals, take our vitamins religiously, get plenty of rest and exercise, et cetera. So you don't have to worry," she said with an encouraging smile. "Your sons are probably the healthiest kids in town."

He didn't look reassured, and Lacey impulsively slid off her stool to stretch up and kiss the taut corner of his mouth. She felt his long release of breath against her cheek and was glad she'd made the gesture.

"We were only separated for three weeks," she said softly. "And they haven't spent a night away from me since then."

Neil moved to lay his cheek against hers and put his arms around her, drawing her between his legs. He didn't speak, but there was a brooding quality to his silence as he held her in a light embrace. She wished he would say something to let her know what he was thinking, and then when he did, she wished he hadn't.

"I guess you wouldn't consider letting me stay tonight," he murmured in her ear, his breath warm and moist.

Lacey's mouth went dry. "I...no, I don't think so," she stammered.

"I could try to convince you," Neil suggested, his voice soft and low. His lips closed on the lobe of her ear and tugged gently, and Lacey twisted her head away.

"Don't," she whispered. "Please, Neil. I'm not ready, and you promised you wouldn't—"

"Will you ever be ready?" he interrupted as he pulled back to look into her eyes. "Be honest, Lacey. Are you just stalling because you don't want to come right out and tell me to take a hike?"

"No!" she denied at once. "I'm not just stalling! I'm still so confused about what I feel. Everything's happened so fast, and I can't afford to make a mistake, especially now that I've got the boys to think of. Can't you give me a little time?"

She thought for a moment that he was going to argue, but then he nodded reluctantly. "Okay. If it's time you need, I'll give it to you. But don't take too long, Lacey. I don't want to just be a visitor in your home. I want us to live together as a family. Now, more than ever. I've already missed so much of my sons' lives, and I don't intend to miss any more if I can help it. When can we tell them? Tomorrow?"

"They have a soccer match at one," she said thoughtfully. "Why don't you come and watch, and then afterward we can all come back here."

Neil agreed, and his mobile mouth slanted crookedly as a thought occurred. "So they play soccer. I'll bet they like pepperoni pizza, too." A speculative look came into his eyes. "That takes care of two of your army of jocks. How about Rosetti the Shrimp? Was he just a smoke screen, too?"

"His name is Paul *Rossi*, he's not a shrimp, and I don't know what you mean by a smoke screen," Lacey retorted. She tried to pull out of his arms, but Neil refused to let her.

"The truth, Lacey! How involved are you with him?"

Irritated and flustered, she evaded a direct answer. "Paul is a very good friend," she said, stressing the "very" a little more than the "friend."

Neil's eyes narrowed, and he increased the pressure of his arms until she had to take a step closer to him. The rough denim of his jeans rubbed her bare thighs, making her unwillingly aware of his lean virility.

"*How* good a friend?" he demanded softly.

"That's none of your business! And let go of me! If you think you can come into *my* house and demand explanations from me, you're wrong!"

"Is he your lover?" Still that soft voice, but now it was lined with steel. Lacey knew he wouldn't let up until she gave him an answer, and she refused to lie! Not even for the sake of her own pride. Her chin went up, her eyes glittering in challenge.

"Not yet," she said distinctly.

She half expected him to call her a liar. Either that or shake her until her teeth rattled. He did neither.

"Why not?" he asked, his voice still soft.

"What?" Lacey wasn't sure she'd heard right.

"Why not? It's sure not for lack of interest on his part. How long have you known him?" The question rapped out so fast Lacey answered without thinking.

"A year. What's that got to do with anything?"

"You've held out for a whole year?"

His skepticism stung her. "I've 'held out' for almost eight!" she snapped, and immediately wanted to rip out her tongue. Her sex life—or lack of it—was no business of his.

She harbored no illusions about Neil's bedroom activities since they'd parted. Knowing his appetites and capacity, she didn't suppose for a minute that he'd lived those years as a monk. For men like Neil, finding willing partners was never a problem. He had it all: looks, money and an animal magnetism that practically oozed from his pores. It had been a prop to her ego to have him think she'd had her share of lovers, too, and at the same time provided a shield, of sorts. She held her breath for his reaction.

"Is that the truth?" he asked, frowning. "In eight years, you've never...." He trailed off, as if the idea was too fantastic to be believed. Lacey grimly decided to brazen it out.

"Slept with a man," she finished for him. "Yes, it's the truth."

"Why?" He sounded both stunned and confused. "A woman like you—you can't tell me men don't approach you constantly."

Lacey finally had to lower her eyes. "You know why, if you'll just think about it," she murmured in a shaky alto.

"I thought it was just me," he said after a long, nerve-racking silence. Then he pulled her to his chest slowly but purposefully. Lacey let her hands rest on his shoulders, neither pushing him away nor returning his embrace, caught between embarrassment and a crazy, fluttery feeling too much like hope to be comfortable.

"Oh, baby, what did I do to you?" Neil sighed into her hair. "Are you that afraid of sex? Of men?"

Lacey somehow knew that it was vitally important to answer honestly, that their entire future—or whether they'd even have one—could depend on what she said next. Her fingers curled against the fabric of his shirt nervously.

"I think...." She faltered, then went on, "I think I'm afraid to find out. It's like when I was a little girl—reason and logic told me there was nothing in the closet at night that hadn't been there during the day; but all the same, if I didn't open the door, whatever was there couldn't jump up and grab me and drag me in with it."

Neil's hands moved slowly over her back, communicating a silent message of understanding. Lacey felt some of her tension drain away under their soothing motion, and her palms once more flattened on his shoulders, feeling the hard ridge of bone and the slight flex of muscle.

"There could be another reason," he suggested silkily. "Maybe you've always known deep down inside that you'd never find what we had with any other man."

Lacey's tone was unexpectedly sarcastic as she answered, "I imagine you'd like to believe that, anyway."

"Yes! You're damned right I would!" Neil said fiercely as his hands suddenly pressed her closer. "It sure beats thinking I turned you into some kind of frigid neurotic!"

"Thanks," she muttered. "You always did have a gift for flattery."

To her surprise his arms relaxed, and she felt his mouth brush her temple in a fleeting caress. "I've come dangerously close to losing my temper several times in the last few minutes," he murmured against her skin, making it tingle pleasurably. "And you've known it. But have you cringed in terror or started to shake like a leaf in the wind?" His rich laugh was pleased, almost exultant. "No! You just keep coming back at me, like a hell-bent little fighter. Lacey, you're fantastic!"

He suddenly moved, shifting his hold to clasp the back of her head as his mouth locked on hers in a hard kiss. Lacey's stomach quivered, though she wasn't sure whether in fear or excitement, and her hands pressed against the cool cotton of his shirt.

"Neil, stop it!" she gasped when he gave her the chance.

"No," he refused calmly. She thought she detected a trace of amusement in his voice and didn't know whether to be more surprised or angry. "Put your arms around my neck."

"I will not!" she retorted, refusing the arrogant command.

"Wanta bet?" Neil murmured, and then before Lacey could twist her head away he reclaimed her mouth.

The old melting warmth stole over her again, weakening her, making her knees and hips feel dangerously loose-jointed. She murmured a halfhearted "No," against his lips, and their pressure increased to shut her up. She held out as long as she could, prolonging his gentle persuasion, and then at last her hands crept slowly over his shoulders to link together at the back of his neck. Neil sighed—a contented, satisfied release of breath—as his arms and hands molded her more fully to him. She felt his arousal, but except for a momentary flicker of unease she wasn't alarmed. Quite the opposite, in fact. The knowledge that he desired her just as much as ever gave her a boost of confidence. Her fingers threaded slowly through his thick hair, her nails raking his scalp as she started to return the kiss.

Neil moaned softly, and then she felt his hand slide beneath her tank top at the waist. His palm glided upward over her smooth torso until his fingers could curve around her breast. His thumb gently teased the nipple while his mouth continued to work its sensual magic, his lips busy, constantly moving over hers, probing and tasting with an enjoyment he didn't try to hide. Lacey was trembling when he finally pulled back a little to look at her flushed face.

"Will you let me stay now?" he whispered huskily.

Lacey gasped for breath. She clung to his neck, afraid she'd fall if she let go. "I can't," she said in an unsteady voice.

His thumb slid across her nipple, making her inhale sharply with pleasure. "You want me, Lacey, as much as I want you," he told her. She could tell he was having to exert quite an effort to control his own voice, and she could feel his heart racing in unison with hers. "Deny it—if you can."

She couldn't, and even if she had, he'd have known she was lying. "Yes, I want you. You know it," she admitted tremulously. "But I can't, Neil. I just can't! It's too soon."

He hesitated briefly, then slid forward on the stool as he forced her into a hard, shockingly intimate contact with his body, his thighs gripping hers while his arms and hands impelled her against him.

"Is this what frightens you?" he asked softly. He pulled at her hips, his hardness a very real threat as he shifted slightly to move against her. "My body, the way it responds whenever I hold you—is that it?"

Lacey had gone rigid. Her palms felt clammy, and there was a buzzing sound in her ears. "Yes," she panted as she strained to pull away from him. "Yes! Neil, please! Don't do this!"

His mouth thinned as he took in her pale face and wide, distressed eyes, but instead of releasing her he moved one arm to her shoulders and pulled her against his chest, so that they were pressed together from collarbone to pelvis.

"It's all right," he told her quietly. "I'm only holding you, Lacey. We're both dressed, and there are four kids within earshot if you decide to call for help. Just let yourself relax. Get used to the feel of me against you again. Let go of the fear and just feel. There's nothing frightening about my body—you know it as well as you know your own."

He kept talking calmly and reasonably, his voice never rising or falling enough to disturb the gradual way he was steadying her nerves.

"There, see," he murmured when her body had relaxed by slow degrees, and she stood passive in his arms. "It's okay. I can hold you so close a flea couldn't get between us, wanting you like crazy the whole time, and still manage to control my raging lust."

He caught Lacey's slight involuntary smile and dropped a kiss on the end of her nose. "Okay?" he asked, and she nodded, looking up at him thoughtfully.

"In the past two hours you've turned my life upside down for the second time," she told him without rancor. "And I'm not sure whether I like it or not."

"How do you think *I* feel?" Neil muttered, a wry twist to his mouth. "I came here with the intention of winning my wife back, and now I find I've got three people to convince instead of one. What are you grinning at?"

Lacey shook her head innocently. "I was just thinking it's just as well you were already gray."

Neil's eyes gleamed between lowered lashes. "That's right, remind me what a decrepit old geezer I am. Just remember, lady, I'm still man enough to handle you."

"That's what I'm afraid of," Lacey said under her breath.

"Don't be." His voice was a throaty caress as he lowered his head. The kiss was meant to be a reassurance, but when Lacey's lips parted under his, Neil's suppressed passion flared to life and became urgent. He pulled away before he lost control, burying his face in her neck. He was breathing hard.

"If I don't get out of here, I'll really give you reason to be afraid," he muttered thickly. He took a deep, slightly ragged breath and then hugged her fiercely before setting her free. "Come on, walk me to the door."

From the front walk Lacey watched him drive away and then went inside to try and sort out her feelings. It seemed inevitable that whenever she and Neil met, they clashed. But the confrontations were becoming less sharp, less painful, and through them they had begun to reach a new understanding of each other. The old wounds, having been exposed, had started to heal. Whether they would ever heal completely, only time would tell.

From the music and occasional outbursts of giggling outside, it would be quite a while before the boys settled down for the night. Lacey made sure the patio door was unlocked and a light was on over the kitchen sink. Little boys, she knew, might need to use the bathroom in the middle of the night, or flee a sudden invasion of slobbering, red-eyed monsters. Then she went down to the family room to take care of the monthly bills.

Her family was in really good shape financially and every other way, she reflected as she stuck a stamp on the last envelope—the Visa payment. She'd started prepaying the principal on the mortgage a couple of years ago and had financed her car through a local bank for tax purposes—she'd needed the interest to deduct—but not because she had to. It was amazing to realize that if she'd wanted, she could have walked into the showroom and written a check for a new car. Absolutely amazing, but, oh, so satisfying after the years of struggling to make ends meet.

She switched on the television to catch the news, then sank onto the couch with a contented sigh. This year had been a good one, so far. The boys had finished second grade with consistently good marks and praise from their teachers for both their scholastic achievements and model behavior. Business had been good—so good, in fact, that she was seriously considering hiring an insurance specialist to share some of the work load she now shouldered alone. Altogether, her life had shaped up very nicely, she thought proudly.

It was also pride that made her want Neil to acknowledge how well she'd done for herself and his sons—to admit that she'd succeeded not only without him but in spite of him. She wanted him to validate her efforts, she realized in surprise, and to endorse her accomplishments. How revolting! Thoroughly disgusted with herself, she turned off the television and the lights and went to bed.

NEIL'S REACTION to his first soccer match was typical of the average father who'd grown up playing and watching football games, Lacey thought in amusement. She'd brought two lawn chairs, but as usual she was only in hers between halves. The rest of the time she was on her feet, cheering for her sons' team at the top of her lungs. Neil looked almost embarrassed to be with her at first, but within fifteen minutes he was at her side, enthusiastic if more than a little confused by some of his sons' antics.

"What the devil was that? Did he do that on purpose?"

"Of course he did it on purpose. It's called 'heading the ball.' They practice it at home all the time."

"Why?" He sounded as if he couldn't believe any normal child would deliberately go around bouncing a ball off his skull, much less practice to perfect the technique.

Lacey chuckled. "I can see we're going to have to give you a few lessons on the basics of soccer," she teased. "That's the glamour shot, and your sons do it better than anybody else their age."

Neil shook his head, but there was a note of pride in his voice as he commented that if they had to participate in such a crazy sport, at least they did seem to be good at it.

Lacey was aware of the curious glances being directed their way as they stood together on the sidelines, but she tried not to let it get to her. Fortunately, she'd at least managed to warn Paul that Neil would be at the match. Sensing her concern that there might be an uncomfortable moment when the two of them came face to face, Paul had acknowledged Neil's presence with a brief nod and then busied himself with his team. Lacey was grateful for his tact, although she suspected he was playing a game of his own that had nothing to do with soccer. Paul's was a waiting game, and his strategy would be to sit back and let the opposition make the first move.

The twins' team won by a score of two to nothing. Todd had scored the first goal and Scott the second, and they were still congratulating each other when they came off the pitch at the end of the match. Lacey wondered if Neil was aware of the speculative looks they gave him as he accompanied them to the parking lot. If so, he gave no sign. He looked very handsome, dressed in a stark white polo shirt and charcoal slacks. But then he always looked handsome. Neil was one of those men whose body made whatever he hung on it look good, though until yesterday she'd never seen him in anything but immaculately tailored clothes.

He followed them home and parked his truck beside Lacey's car in the drive. The boys looked at him again and then at each other as they walked to the house, exchanging a silent message Lacey was at a loss to interpret. They were unnaturally quiet as she led the way into the kitchen to pour everyone a glass of iced tea. She turned from the counter to find them staring at her, and their utterly solemn expressions took her by surprise. She frowned a little as she carried the tray holding the glasses to the table. Neil came from the doorway, where he'd been lounging with his hands in his pockets, to stand close beside her. He gave her a questioning look, and Lacey shrugged a response. Something was definitely in the air. The boys usually talked a blue streak after a match, and they were always ready for a cold drink. Now they stood like a pair of small statues regarding the two adults.

"Todd? Scott?" she asked with motherly concern. "Is anything wrong?"

"No," said Scott.

"We're just waiting," added Todd.

"Waiting?" she repeated in puzzlement.

"For the talk," Scott explained.

Lacey was growing more confused by the minute. "The talk? What talk?"

"You know, mom." Todd glanced up at Neil, who looked no more enlightened than Lacey. "The one where you tell us who he is."

Her eyes flew to Neil in startled surprise. Before she could think of a response he motioned her to keep silent and dropped into a chair to put himself closer to eye level with the twins.

"Who do you think I am?" he asked softly.

They exchanged an uncertain look, then took turns answering.

"Well, we're not sure . . . ."

"But we think maybe . . . ."

"You might be . . . ."

And then together, "Our dad."

Lacey was stunned, absolutely flabbergasted. How did they guess?

Neil leaned forward, resting his arms on his knees as he studied their faces closely. "And how would you feel about it if I said I was?" he asked, his tone guarded and low.

"Oh, we'd like it!" Scott answered at once. "Right, Todder?"

"Right," Todd confirmed with a nod. "We already talked about it, and we decided you'd be a neat dad, even if you don't know much about putting up tents. You're funny," he elaborated with an impish grin.

Lacey decided it was time she got into the act. "Hold on a minute here. *When* did you talk about it? And what made you think Neil was your father in the first place?"

"Oh, that's easy," Todd answered. "We saw you kissing each other."

"Last night," Scott put in, "through the window."

They both turned to Neil. "See, mom doesn't go around kissing guys much," Scott told him seriously.

"Anyway, not like *that*!"

"So we knew you were somebody special."

"And who's more special than a dad?"

Neil looked up at Lacey, his eyes twinkling. "You can't fault their logic," he drawled.

"*Are* you?" Todd had become impatient with waiting for an answer. Neil glanced back at the boys, and the wistful appeal on their faces sobered him instantly.

"Yes," he said softly. "I'm your father." There was a roughness to his voice that didn't escape Lacey, and she swallowed hard, her throat suddenly tight.

The twins turned to each other, ear-to-ear smiles breaking out on their faces.

"We were right!"

"I knew it all the time."

And then Neil's slightly wary look of expectancy changed to amazement as they simultaneously hurled themselves at him. They started out standing between his legs, but within seconds each had claimed a knee and they were fastened around his neck like leeches.

"They're very affectionate," Lacey said when Neil's questioning eyes sought hers. She smiled and saw his instant relief. With a small shock she realized he'd been worried that she might resent his sons' immediate and enthusiastic acceptance of him. Unaccountably, the knowledge brought sudden tears to her eyes, but before Neil could notice, the boys were bombarding him with questions.

"Are you gonna live here with us now?"

"No." His gaze flicked briefly to Lacey. "I've just bought a farm out in the country."

"A *farm*! Neat-o! Has it got pigs and chickens?"

"And cows? A farm's supposed to have cows."

"And horses!"

"Yeah, *horses*! Has it got horses, dad?"

Lacey saw him gulp at that, but his voice was steady enough when he answered. "I'm afraid it doesn't have any of those things. At least, not yet. See, it's an old farm and nobody's lived on it for quite a while. It needs a lot of fixing up."

"Can we help? We can hammer nails real good."

"Yeah, if we helped, you could get it fixed up quicker, and then you could get some horses."

Neil struggled to contain a grin as he looked from

one of them to the other. "Can you really handle a hammer?" he asked somberly.

They both nodded vigorously, and he pursed his lips in thought. "Okay, then. You can be my chief carpenters. We'll work out with mom when you can come out and start fixing up the barn. It'll need new stalls if we're gonna have horses."

The promise earned him two ecstatic hugs from the boys and a not altogether approving look from Lacey. He lifted his brows as if to say, *How can I resist them?* And her expression answered clearly, *You'd better learn.*

Neil stayed for dinner and on until the boys' bedtime, at their insistence. When he bent over their bunks to kiss them good-night they locked their arms around his neck for a tight hug.

"You'll come back tomorrow, like you promised, won't you?" Todd asked anxiously.

Neil sat on the edge of his bed and gently gave the little boy the reassurance he needed. "I'll be here," he murmured, his voice unusually deep. "You just make sure you're up bright and early, and wear some old clothes, so mom won't get too mad at us if they get dirty. Okay?"

Todd nodded with a grin. "Okay. Night, dad."

"Night, Todder. Goodnight, Scotty. Now you two get to sleep. I'll see you in the morning."

When Lacey finished tucking them in she found him downstairs, gazing at their framed school pictures on a table in the living room. He looked up when she entered, then held out a hand.

"Come here," he said huskily. "I need to hold you."

Lacey walked into his arms without a second's hesitation. He held her tightly, his cheek pressed against the top of her head. She knew he was struggling with emotions he had never before experienced and was trying to cope with. Her hands moved over his back in a gently soothing rhythm.

"They're so amazing!" He shook his head in wonder. "They just accepted me! No questions about where I'd been until now, no resentment about the way I just showed up. I don't *deserve* two kids like that."

"I know the feeling," she answered softly. "Sometimes I look at them and can't believe they're really mine. But you done good," she murmured, knowing he needed some reassurance of his own, but wouldn't ask for it.

"You really think so?" he said as he held her away a little.

"Mm-hmm. Except for the bit about the horses," she added. "*Horses*, Neil?"

His mouth slanted upward at one corner. "Well . . . how about a couple of ponies then, until they're big enough for horses?"

"I don't want you spoiling them," she warned sternly.

"Who, me?" His air of innocence didn't fool Lacey for a minute, and her expression showed it. Neil released a sigh. "Okay, I promise not to go overboard on the presents. Besides," he added in a sexy murmur as he bent to kiss her neck, "I'd just as soon spoil their mother."

"I won't be bought with expensive trinkets," she

quipped to cover her reaction to his caressing lips and tongue.

"Actually, what I had in mind wouldn't cost a cent." His deep voice was muffled against her skin, and Lacey couldn't suppress the shiver that ran down her back. "You might say it's the gift that goes on giving. Am I stimulating your curiosity at all?"

He was stimulating a lot more than her curiosity, but she forced herself to push him away with a bland little smile.

"Sorry, not interested," she said lightly. "Hadn't you better be getting home? You've got quite a day ahead of you tomorrow."

Neil frowned, then observed her heightened color. The warmth returned to his eyes as he said, "Okay, I'll go...for now." He added softly, "Sure you don't want to come with us in the morning?"

Lacey shook her head. "I think you should have some time alone with them. It'll give you a chance to get to know one another."

"You trust me with them but not with you." There was more than a trace of bitterness in his voice.

Lacey dropped her head to conceal the conflicting emotions it roused in her. "Please, Neil," she murmured wearily. "Don't—"

He reached out suddenly, taking her in his arms. "I *love* you, Lacey!" he said fiercely. "If it takes the rest of my life, I'll make you believe that!"

As he crushed her lips in a kiss so violent it took her breath away, Lacey found to her surprise that she wanted to return it with an equal intensity. Maybe it was the fact that he had taken her by surprise, but whatever the reason, when she realized how shamelessly she was kissing him back, she wrenched her mouth away in horror. This time it was her own response that had frightened her, but Neil couldn't know that. He held her against him for a moment more, and then his arms dropped to his sides.

"I didn't intend to do that," he said heavily. "Are you all right?"

Lacey nodded, avoiding his eyes. "Yes. But I wish you'd leave now."

"All right." His shoulders seemed to slump as he turned for the door. He looked back with his hand on the knob. "I'll be here around eight, if that's okay."

"Fine," Lacey agreed. "I'll have the boys ready."

Neil nodded once, and then he was gone, closing the door silently behind him. As soon as she heard his truck start, Lacey sank into a chair She was trembling, weak and shaky, and the worst thing was she knew that the reason for her delayed reaction wasn't fear. It was something much more threatening to her peace of mind.

7

NEIL BROUGHT the same single-minded determination to parenting that had made him such a success in business. Within a week he started arriving at Lacey's house during the day, relieving Mrs. Moore to take charge of the boys himself. Lacey wondered how he managed to get anything done at the farm with them underfoot all the time, but then she supposed he wasn't actually doing any of the physical labor himself, anyway. So far as she knew, Neil didn't know the first thing about carpentry or plumbing, and he could well afford to hire the best people around to do whatever needed doing. He must be spending a lot of time outdoors, though. At the end of the week he was almost as brown as the twins, and while she couldn't tell that he'd gained any weight, he looked somehow harder, fitter in the jeans and work shirt she'd grown used to by now.

The boys adored him. Every night she was subjected to a litany of, "Dad said this," and "Dad said that," during dinner and during bedtime preparations. It occurred to her that she might be forgiven a twinge of jealousy now and then, but strangely there was none. She could only feel happiness and gratitude that they finally had their father around; and as for Neil, he obviously took such joy in them that she was happy for him, too.

Lacey's work kept her so busy that she seldom saw him except in passing. If he had the boys in the afternoon, he always called to see when she planned to leave the office and was waiting when she got home. He refused when she invited him to stay and eat with them, and Lacey didn't insist. She suspected he was giving her some space, some time to decide about their own relationship while he concentrated on the developing one with his sons. For the time being at least, he seemed content with getting to know them and making up for all the time he'd missed with them. He even took them to a soccer practice, a fact Lacey didn't know about until later, when Paul stopped by the office to invite her to lunch.

"We missed you at practice yesterday," he remarked as they faced each other across a booth in a downtown restaurant.

"Oh, no! I completely forgot!" Lacey exclaimed in dismay. "I've just been so busy lately. But I'm surprised one of the boys didn't remind me. They never forget a practice."

"They didn't forget this one," Paul said dryly. "Their father brought them."

"What?" She was astonished. "Neil took them to practice?"

"And stayed until it was over. I got the feeling he was checking me out—sizing up the competition, you might say."

"Oh, Paul, I'm sorry," Lacey apologized in embarrassment. "He once referred to you as 'the competition' but I guess I didn't really take him seriously."

"Don't apologize," Paul said with a laugh. "If our positions were reversed, I'd have done the same thing. But you know something? If he wasn't your husband, I think I could easily get to like him."

Lacey gaped at him in surprise. "You're not serious, are you?"

"Absolutely. He is what is known as a man's man. I think you would always know exactly where you stood with him. He isn't the type to play games or say things he does not mean." Paul leaned forward, frowning slightly. "He is also a man who does not possess an unlimited amount of patience, Lacey. From what you've told me, I gather he wants to resume your marriage, and I also gather that you are reluctant to commit yourself. Tell me to shut up and mind my own business, if you want."

She shook her head, her eyes on her fingers as they played with the table setting in front of her. "No. I gave you the right to comment when I confided in you, and if you have something to say, I'd like to hear it."

"All right, then, here it is," Paul said quietly. "I think you are being unfair to him, Lacey."

Her head shot up incredulously. "Unfair to *him*!" she echoed in disbelief.

"Yes. I don't know what happened to drive you apart, and I don't want to know. It's none of my business," he said when she started to speak. "I do know that he hurt you very badly, and that you've carried around a lot of bitterness and pain because of it for eight long years. But, Lacey, you cannot carry a grudge for the rest of your life. Anyone who watches him with his sons can see how much he cares for them, how important it is to him to be a good father to them—"

"I don't deny that," Lacey interrupted. "I know he's good with them, and they love him, Paul." She shook her head wonderingly. "I didn't think it could be possible for them to accept him so totally and so quickly, but they have. And I'm glad, truly I am. But his relationship with them has nothing to do with how *I* feel about him. They only know the Neil Hartmann they met a week ago, but I remember the other one, the one who could be hard and brutal and totally unscrupulous in his dealings with other people."

"And you find it impossible to believe that he has changed, that he is no longer that man?" Paul suggested with a trace of impatience. "Stranger things have happened, Lacey. Years have passed since you knew that Neil Hartmann. Who can say what might have happened to change him in that time. You are letting bad memories cloud your judgment. The man I saw yesterday might occasionally be hard, but I cannot imagine him being brutal or unscrupulous."

He sat back with a sigh, as if he had said more than he intended and was slightly irritated with himself for becoming so involved in someone else's problems.

"I am only giving you my opinion as a man, and nothing more. It appears to me that he has been honest in telling you what he wants, what he expects, and I think you owe him the courtesy of being equally honest with him. If you have no intention of becoming involved with him again, tell him so and be done with it."

Lacey looked at him curiously, her eyes narrowed. "All right, since you're pushing honesty, let me ask *you* something, Paul," she said slowly. "If I sent Neil packing, so to speak, exactly where would that leave you and me?"

His shrug was eloquent as a charming smile curved his well-shaped mouth. "I have never deceived you about what *I* want, either, Lacey. I would like to have an affair with you, but I'm not ready for marriage or the kind of commitment it requires. Perhaps someday, when I have done all I want to do, seen all I want to see, but not for the present. Does that answer your question?"

Lacey's lips pursed as she contained a smile. "Perfectly," she said in a dry tone.

"And now you are disappointed in me?"

"Not at all," she denied. "You are what you are, and you've never deceived me. I just wanted to get it out in the open so there wouldn't be any mistake or misunderstanding. You see, Paul, I *need* the kind of commitment you talk about. I know myself well enough to know a casual affair isn't for me—not with you or anyone else. If I can't have it all, I'd rather do without."

Paul spread his hands, palms up. "It appears we must agree to disagree," he said with another smile. "A pity, because we go well together, you and I. I suspect I will end up envying that husband of yours when he succeeds in winning you back."

"*If*, not when," Lacey corrected. But she had the

distinct feeling that for him the fact that she and Neil would eventually get back together was a forgone conclusion.

She wasn't sure whether she was more annoyed or stung by Paul's assumptions when she returned to the office. She'd known he was biding his time, waiting for her to clarify exactly what her relationship with Neil would be from now on. But apparently in the meantime he'd come to see the whole situation from Neil's point of view. And what's more, he seemed to be siding with Neil against her!

The very idea left her feeling confused and unsettled. Paul was a very perceptive man, usually right on target in his assessments of other people's characters and motivations. Normally she wouldn't have doubted his insight, but in this case her own feelings were too ambivalent to allow her to be objective.

She had a full work load that day: she'd shown three houses, settled two insurance claims and sold a new homeowner's policy. There were also the usual number of telephone inquiries, mail to read and answer and a meeting with two attorneys concerning possible litigation against a teenager who'd bought auto insurance from her and then proceeded to drive his VW Rabbit across a neighbor's lawn and into the side of his house. Busy as she was, however, she kept coming back to that disturbing conversation at lunch.

She was still thinking about the things Paul had said when she arrived home that evening. The boys were there, along with Mrs. Moore, who had dinner started. Lacey thanked her sincerely. She had a Business and Professional Women's Club meeting that night, and she was already running late.

"Yes, and I'm so sorry I won't be able to sit, but everything's worked out all right, after all," Mrs. Moore commented as she collected her purse from the coat closet.

Lacey looked up from the sofa, where she was removing her shoes. "You can't sit tonight?"

"No, I'm afraid not. Remember, I told you last week that my niece and her husband were going to be in town, and I'd asked them to dinner."

"Oh, no, I forgot," Lacey sighed. Then, in resignation, "Well, I guess I'll just stay home."

"Oh, but that's not necessary," Mrs. Moore said in surprise. "Didn't the boys tell you when you came in? They called their father, and he's coming to stay with them. Now I really do have to run, or my own dinner won't get cooked. I'll see you Monday morning."

After she left, Lacey tracked the boys down in the back yard, where they were kicking a soccer ball around.

"Did you guys call your dad and ask him to take care of you tonight?" she accused with a frown.

Todd picked up the ball and they both came to where she was standing on the patio. "Sure, Mom. We knew he wouldn't care. Are you mad cause we didn't ask you first?"

"Mad? No, I'm not *mad*," she denied. "It's just that I don't think we should impose on him. He's had you out at the farm every day this week, and he might want a little time to himself. For all we know, he might have already had plans for tonight."

"He didn't," Scott refuted. "He said he was just sitting around reading a boring book about spies and shady ladies."

"What's a shady lady, anyway?" Todd asked curiously.

"Never mind! How did you know where to call him in the first place? Did he tell you what motel he was staying in? Maybe I can catch him there and tell him he doesn't have to come."

They both gave her exasperated looks.

"Dad's not staying at any motel," Scott said patiently.

"Why would he do that, when he's got such a neat house?" Todd pointed out.

"You mean he's been staying out at the farm all this time!" Lacey exclaimed in amazement. "Good grief, the place is a wreck! There isn't even any furniture— not even a bed, for Pete's sake!"

"He doesn't need one."

"He's got a sleeping bag."

She tried to summon up a picture of Neil stretched out on a bare wood floor in the big old farmhouse, rolled up in a sleeping bag, but it was impossible.

"Mom?" Scott spoke up tentatively. "He really did say he'd be glad to come in and stay with us. Do you have to tell him not to?"

Lacey looked down at the appeal on the two faces raised to her and wavered in indecision. *Be honest,* she told herself. *You just don't want Neil to get a toe-*

hold in this house. You're afraid he'll move in, and you won't be able to get him out again.

"Oh, all right," she began to capitulate, but the peal of the doorbell inside interrupted before she could finish.

The boys dashed past her to answer it, and by the time Lacey pulled the sliding patio door shut behind her they were dragging Neil into the dinette. He was laughing at something Scott had just said when he suddenly looked up and their eyes met. Lacey felt a tightness in her chest and throat as the smile slowly left his face and something much more intense appeared in his eyes.

"Hi," he said softly. "Sitter's here."

"I'm sorry to inconvenience you like this, especially on such short notice," she said awkwardly. There was nothing she could do about the huskiness in her voice; she just hoped Neil wouldn't notice it, or if he did he wouldn't guess the reason for it. "I didn't know they'd called you until I got home."

"It's no inconvenience," he denied, then grinned down at the boys, who beamed back at him. "Besides, I owe these two for the work they've put in this week." He looked back at Lacey, one brow lifting in question. "What time does your meeting start?"

She glanced at her watch. "In half an hour. If I don't hurry, I'll be late. Their supper's in the oven, and they know where everything else is. There should be plenty, in case you haven't eaten."

She walked past him to go collect her shoes from the living room and heard him tell the boys to start getting out plates and silverware. *He's learning*, she thought in amusement, and a small smile curved her lips as she straightened with the shoes in her hand. Neil was standing in the living-room door, frowning.

"You look bushed," he said flatly.

"I am," Lacey replied as she sat down to pull her shoes on again.

"Then why don't you skip this hen party and stay home?"

"This 'hen party'—" she bristled "—happens to be with a group of businesswomen who are working to improve the quality of our community services. And as I happen to be the president," she continued angrily, "I can hardly stay home just because I'm a little tired. How many meetings have *you* missed with the excuse that you'd already put in a long day?"

"That's different," Neil claimed. "I had a business to run, and it was important to keep up my contacts."

"Will you listen to yourself!" Lacey rose in her anger to face him. "What do you think *I'm* doing, Neil, flitting around town like some kind of social butterfly? *I* run a business, too, in case it's slipped your mind. *I* also earn a very respectable living, and I support two children and make the payments on this house and that car sitting in the driveway. I strongly resent the implication that because I'm a woman, nothing I do can be taken seriously. Do you think I'm just playing at being a grown-up, Neil, dressing up in high heels and trotting off to work every day just to fill the time between tea parties and bridge games?"

"No, of course that's not what I think." Neil ran an impatient hand through his hair. "But like you said, you've got two children to raise, and how much time do you get to spend with them? I'll bet you've seen them altogether less than an hour today, Lacey, and God knows how much this week. If you're not at the office, you're off at some committee meeting or showing a piece of real estate to a potential buyer."

Her lips clamped together, a sign of her cold fury. "Are you saying you consider me a bad mother, Neil?" she demanded curtly. "Do you actually have the gall to stand there and accuse me of neglecting my children? The poor little things seem deprived to you, do they?" Her short laugh revealed her irritation. "You really are something. I've been both mother and father to them for more than seven years, and suddenly *you're* the expert on child rearing!"

Tears of anger glistened in her eyes, but beneath the outrage she was deeply hurt. Did he think she wouldn't *like* to have more time to spend with the boys? She snatched at every available minute, trying to cram as much as she could into what time they did have together, but she knew that the necessity of providing for them had cheated her of many priceless moments that could never be recaptured. Still, that didn't give Neil the right to criticize. While she had been slaving and worrying about the bills, doing the best she could under sometimes rotten conditions, he had been blithely ignorant of his sons' very existence, going his own merry way in comfort and luxury.

"I'm not setting myself up as any kind of expert," he said quietly. "And I certainly wouldn't ever accuse you of being a bad mother, Lacey. Considering the odds against you, it's a miracle the boys have turned out so well adjusted and happy. You've done a terrific job with them, and I know it hasn't been easy. But, dammit!" he suddenly swore with surprising vehemence. "There are more important things than career success and the selfish kind of gratification that comes with it! Prestige and respect don't take the place of human warmth and affection, and all the money in the world is cold comfort when you look around and realize it's all you've got to show for your life—that if you died tomorrow, there wouldn't be a soul whose life would be affected for more than a couple of weeks!"

Lacey stared at him in stunned silence. Was this Neil Hartmann talking? The same Neil Hartmann who'd been so busy running his company that he hadn't even had time for a honeymoon? The Neil Hartmann who ate lunch at his desk when he bothered to eat at all, because he couldn't spare half an hour to go out?

She shook her head in bewilderment. "I know all that, Neil."

"Do you? Do you, really, Lacey?" His voice shook with intensity.

"Yes. I do. I'm not obsessed with my job, it's just that I *have* to spend a lot of time at it. But at least twice a year I take off for a week and let Rick run things so the boys and I can get away together. They mean more to me than any career ever could," she told him sincerely.

"I guess I knew that. It's just . . . ." Neil looked up at her suddenly, the undisguised appeal in his eyes causing Lacey's breathing to falter.

"Lacey," he began, and the yearning in his voice combined with the heartfelt look he was giving her were more than her already frayed nerves could take. She was suddenly afraid—not in a physical sense, but of the demands she sensed he was about to make on her emotionally. She quickly glanced at her watch and used the time as an excuse to flee his disturbing presence.

AFTER THE DAY she'd already put in and then the angry confrontation with Neil, Lacey expected to have a thoroughly rotten time at the meeting. True, she didn't arrive in the best of moods, but as they worked their way down the agenda and she was reminded of all the positive work this group had done for the community, her spirits lifted.

Darn him—she wished he could be at this "hen party" to see and hear for himself exactly what could be accomplished by a group of dedicated, hardworking women! But of course he wasn't here, because he'd stayed home to watch his sons—*their* sons, she amended with an involuntary inner softening.

They loved him so much, and it was obvious to anyone who cared to look that he was absolutely crazy about them. There was such joy in his eyes when they rested on his children, and sometimes a wondering, almost awestruck delight, as if he could hardly believe they were really his. He hung on their every word, watched them as if he'd never get his fill, finding excuses to touch them. The boys weren't nearly so reticent. They needed no excuse to throw themselves at his legs or climb onto his lap, small arms fastening around him tightly.

Lacey smiled softly to herself, feeling the relaxing deep down inside her, unaware of the speculative looks her almost madonnalike expression was drawing from the other women. If she'd happened to catch sight of her own reflection in a mirror at that moment, she'd have been stunned by what her luminous eyes and gently curved lips gave away.

It was almost nine when she returned home. The sound of the television led her downstairs to the family room, and she stopped in the doorway, her eyes misting at the sight before her.

Neil sat on the couch, each of his arms around a pajama-clad twin snuggled up against him in sleep. Scott had climbed onto his lap, and Todd's compact little body was arranged in a position that could only be comfortable for a child, his legs stretched out to one side while his upper body leaned against his father's chest. Lacey came quietly into the room and Neil looked up, a smile lighting his eyes as he saw her.

"What's this, a slumber party?" she whispered in amusement.

"Don't blame them for not being in bed," he whispered back. "It's not their fault their old man's a pushover. How'd the meeting go?"

"Fine." It struck Lacey how silly it was to be conducting a conversation in whispers, and she grinned. "We got a lot accomplished." She perched on the arm of the couch to remove her shoes and wiggle her toes with a heartfelt sigh of relief. "Come on, you take Scotty and I'll get Todd."

"No, stay there," Neil said as he eased away from Todd, and the boy slumped onto the cushions. "I'll come back for him."

Lacey shook her head. "I'm used to carrying them."

After the boys had been put to bed he took her hand and led her back to the family room.

"Sit there," he ordered, indicating the couch. "I've kept your dinner warm."

Lacey sank gratefully onto the plump sofa cushions as Neil left the room. He came back a few minutes later bearing a TV tray with a serving of Mrs. Moore's tuna casserole and a bowl of salad, along with two glasses of iced tea. He sipped at one to keep her company while she ate, then took the tray back to the kitchen.

When he returned he casually took a seat beside her and then just as casually reached down to draw her feet onto his lap. Lacey tensed slightly with nervousness, but he only started to gently but firmly massage her aching feet.

"Women have got to be idiots to wear those things," he muttered, nodding at the high-heeled sandals she'd left lying on the floor. "It's a wonder you don't break your neck, staggering around on those stilts."

"Women have always sacrificed comfort for fashion," she agreed ruefully, "and probably always will. Oh, that feels good." She sighed deliciously.

"What you need's a tub of hot water to soak 'em in," Neil suggested, then suddenly grinned, surprising her.

"What's so funny?"

"Oh, I was just thinking. Do you realize how much like an old married couple we sound? First that argument before you left, and just now? Only the thing is I get the feeling I'm coming off more like the nagging wife, and you do a dandy impression of a hassled husband."

"You're right," she admitted. "The way you lit into me about not spending enough time with the kids *did* sound just like a nagging wife. And when I came in, you asked me how my meeting went."

"I even brought you supper in front of the TV," Neil reminded her, his eyes twinkling.

"So you did. I never thought I'd live to see the day," Lacey teased. "Neil Hartmann, househusband. Next thing I know, you'll be doing the laundry and making the beds."

"Don't hold your breath," he muttered as his hands shifted upward to knead the tensed muscles of her calves. "But I am sorry I was so rough on you before." He gave her a regretful smile. "The problem is, *I* want to be the one to take care of you all. I'd like you to be dependent on *me* as provider, but I'm beginning to realize that's just not possible. You've been on your own too long to just turn yourself over to somebody else."

"Do you really understand that, Neil?" Lacey asked softly. "Have you really come that far, that you can appreciate what my independence means to me? Can you accept the fact that I can take care of myself and the boys, and the pride it gives me?"

"I think so," he murmured, then smiled crookedly.

"I'm not saying I *like* it, but I do accept it. The trouble is, if I can't buy you with a pampered life of luxury, what the hell am I supposed to use to convince you you'd be better off with me than without me?"

Lacey suddenly felt poised on the brink of something enormous, something that could change her whole life. A wild kind of exhilaration pulsed through her veins and shimmered in her eyes as they met his.

"What makes you think you need to offer anything more than yourself?" she asked in a husky whisper.

Neil's eyes dropped, but not before she saw the discouraged look in them. "I'm not about to con myself into believing that would be enough," he said harshly. "The last time, I—"

Lacey impulsively laid a hand on his arm to cut him off. "That was then, Neil," she told him softly. "This is now."

His head came up slowly. His eyes were guarded, cautious as they searched hers. He didn't speak, and Lacey was glad. Words might have shattered the fragile, almost magical spell she could feel weaving its way around them. He leaned toward her slowly—almost *too* slowly—until their lips were only an inch apart, and she could feel his warm breath on her face. Lacey knew the next move was up to her. With only a momentary flutter of apprehension, she made it, closing the distance between them. When she opened her eyes they were both lying on the couch, face to face. One of Neil's arms was under her, holding her close against him, and his other hand was tenderly stroking her face. He brushed soft kisses across her

cheeks and forehead, then pulled back to look deep
into her eyes.

"Are you afraid?"

Lacey moved her head in denial. "Nervous,
though," she admitted, and her tongue came out to
moisten her lips, as if to give proof.

Neil's finger touched where her tongue had been.
"That's a very provocative, very sexy gesture, did
you know that?" he murmured with a soft, heart-
tugging smile.

Her eyes widened anxiously. "N-no. I wasn't trying to be provocative, or . . . ."

"Shh, I was only teasing. And don't be nervous.
There's no reason to be."

"Easy for you to say," Lacey replied with some
embarrassment. *How ridiculous to be shy about
lying in your own husband's arms*, she thought.
The trouble was, she didn't think of him as her husband anymore; he didn't even *feel* like her husband.

Neil's smile warmed, his eyes crinkling at the corners. "You can joke. That's a good sign. Now don't
panic," as he gently put both arms around her, "but
I'm going to kiss you. I mean *really* kiss you, like I've
been wanting to ever since I got here tonight and saw
you standing there in the doorway in your bare feet."

His mouth is so warm, so firm, so perfect, Lacey
thought as her hands reached up to clasp his head;
and then sensation crowded out all thought as she
whirled weightless in a vortex of feeling, the strength
of Neil's arms the only security she needed or wanted. She was trembling when he finally eased his

mouth from hers to plant several light kisses over her face and neck.

"Oh, I've missed that," he breathed in her ear, and a shiver raced through her in response. "Baby, you're shaking!"

There was such a wealth of self-reproach in his deep voice that Lacey hurried to reassure him. "It's all right. I admit I'm a little shook up, but I can handle it," she told him with a trace of dry humor.

"Sure?" Neil asked in concern, and when she nodded he kissed her again, very softly, as he shifted a little to pillow her head with his shoulder. "Okay then, we'll just lie here for a while, just like this. Are you comfortable?"

"Physically or mentally?" Lacey quipped, and his arms contracted slightly as he dropped another kiss onto the top of her head.

"I love you so much." He sounded so sincere, so...*humble*, that Lacey's breath caught, and she felt the sting of tears. Neil immediately looked down at her, the concern in his clouded eyes intensifying the rush of emotion his words had generated.

"What's wrong?" he asked sharply.

Lacey's smile was a bit unsteady as she shook her head. "N-nothing. It's just that I think I'm actually starting to believe you."

Neil's hand trembled as he pressed her head to his chest, and his voice was rough with emotion. "Believe it, because it's the truth!" He paused a moment to regain control, then grinned crookedly as he asked, "Would it help convince you if you kept hearing it over and over?" And then, before she could answer, he started telling her, interspersing his words with kisses that were too brief to do more than whet her appetite. "There, that should do it for a while," he murmured as he settled her against his chest again.

"You really take a girl by storm, don't you?" Lacey said shakily as she nestled closer.

"I can only hope," Neil drawled. They lay silently for a while, and then he uttered a soft oath under his breath.

"What?" Lacey mumbled drowsily.

"I forgot to tell you. Mrs. Moore called while you were out. Her niece is going home to Chicago tomorrow, and they've invited her to come stay with them for a week or so. I told her to go and have a nice visit."

"You what?" Lacey was suddenly wide awake. "Neil, I'll never find somebody else to stay with the boys on such short notice!"

"What about Neil Hartmann, househusband?" he said with a grin.

Lacey started to tell him he must be out of his mind, then reconsidered. She chewed her lower lip, and her eyes narrowed to hide their shrewd gleam.

"Do you realize what you'd be letting yourself in for? Mrs. Moore doesn't just keep an eye on them while I'm at work. She usually gives them their breakfast and lays out their clothes, and she also fixes lunch every day. And if I'm going to be late, she starts dinner for me."

"You don't think I could manage?" he challenged.

"I didn't say that. Could you?" she countered.

"There's no doubt in my mind," Neil replied confidently. Lacey smothered a smile as he swung his long legs off the couch and pulled her up to sit beside him. "You're about to conk out. Get yourself off to bed, woman. I'll let myself out. Oh, and I won't be around tomorrow," he said as he got to his feet. Lacey rose to stand beside him, tipping her head back to look up at him.

"Need a day to rest up before you start your new job?" she teased.

"No, it just so happens I have some personal business to take care of," he replied vaguely.

Despite his claim that he could let himself out, Lacey walked him to the front door, Neil's arm around her shoulders, and hers linking her to his waist. As much as twenty-four hours ago she'd have felt uncomfortable, maybe even threatened, by such closeness, but now it seemed perfectly natural.

"By the way, did I mention that Bob Anderson will be here one day next week?" Neil asked as they reached the entryway.

"Bob will?" Lacey's voice held pleasure. Bob had been Neil's personal assistant almost from the day he'd gone into business, and she'd gotten along well with him on the few occasions they'd met.

"Mm-hmm. He's bringing some paperwork I need to look over. I imagine he'll only stay the day. He's handling the transition period for me while the new management takes over."

"I'm surprised you didn't want to supervise that yourself," Lacey remarked, and his lazy smile spoke volumes even before he answered.

"I'd originally intended to, but after that first trip

back here I suddenly had more important things on my mind," he reminded her gently.

He drew Lacey into his arms, and her hands quite naturally lifted to his chest, then slid over his shoulders and around his neck.

"I'm proud of your restraint," she told him. "You haven't dropped one hint about spending the night."

Neil's smile came through in his voice. "I figured I'd better not push my luck, that's all. Don't think for a minute it hasn't been on my mind." Then his voice deepened and grew serious. "You took a big step tonight, Lacey, and I'm grateful."

"Don't be," she said with a touch of wry humor. "To be honest, I was thinking of myself as much as of you."

"I hope you mean that, baby." He inhaled deeply, then looked down at her with a bittersweet smile. "It's like being sent into exile, leaving the three of you to go out to that empty old barn. Give me something to take with me, Lacey, something to keep me warm for a while."

She stretched up on tiptoe, pulling his head down as her eyes closed and her lips parted invitingly. Neil's arms immediately tightened, while his mouth and tongue worked their sensual magic until she was responding mindlessly. When he finally released her they were both trembling.

"I'd better get out of here before I forget my good intentions again," he said roughly. "What time do you want me here Monday morning?"

Lacey's lips twitched as she told him, "Between seven A.M. and a quarter after."

"Seven! Good grief, what time do you go to work?"

"I open for business at precisely eight o'clock. Of course, if you don't think you can be up that early—"

"I'll be here," Neil muttered with a frown. "Somehow I get the feeling I've been suckered . . . by a master."

"It was your idea to take over for Mrs. Moore," Lacey reminded him, "and after all, you are the one who told her to go visit her niece."

"All right, all right! Seven!" he repeated glumly. "Nobody goes to work that early. It's practically the middle of the night."

He was still grumbling when Lacey, with an amused grin, pushed him out the door and closed it behind him. The coming week should test his resolve to the limit. If he was still determined to be a family man by the end of it, she thought she just might be willing to accommodate him.

8

THEY ARGUED more during the following week than in all the time they'd known each other.

Monday it was over the state of the house when Lacey got home from work.

"It looks like a pigsty," she fumed as she stalked around the family room. "What did you do, spend the whole day seeing how big a mess you could make in this one room?"

"It's not that bad," Neil claimed with a scowl. "And we've only been here a couple of hours. We spent most of the afternoon at the farm."

"Neil, Hurricane Hilda couldn't wreak this much havoc in just a couple of hours," she snorted as she flung a mud-splattered size-eight T-shirt at him. He caught it in one hand, his brows drawing together.

"You're really in a foul mood," he muttered. "Okay, maybe you had a rotten day, but that's no reason—"

"My day was just fine until I got home," Lacey snapped. "How would *you* like to come home to this?" Her hand swept the cluttered room in one disgusted gesture, taking in the clothes draped over furniture, toys, shoes and tube socks littering the floor, and sweating Snoopy glasses leaving rings on the tables.

Neil shifted uneasily under her accusing glare. "All right, I admit it could be a little neater." He ignored Lacey's hoot of disbelief at such a blatant understatement. "But I still say it's not as bad as you're making out. You're nit-picking. I think I did really well for the first day."

"Oh, you do, do you?" Lacey challenged with one hand on her hip.

"Listen, lady," Neil's temper rose to match hers. "The boys weren't even fed or dressed when you left this morning!"

"I distinctly remember telling you they might not be," Lacey countered. "This is their summer vacation, Neil. Why do you suppose I have a sitter come *here*? If I'm going to drag them out of bed at the crack of dawn and have them fed and dressed by seven-thirty, I might as well take them to a day-care center, and then they wouldn't get to see their friends all day."

She took a deep breath and tried to bring her irritation under control.

"What did you give them for lunch?"

"Tomato soup and grilled cheese sandwiches." The answer was curt. Neil wasn't used to being spoken to like an employee who'd been called on the carpet; in his experience, the shoe had always been on the other foot.

"Did you eat here or at the farm?" Lacey asked in a more conciliatory tone. Maybe she *had* been a little rough on him. After all, this was a whole new experience for him.

"Here. The kitchen's not quite finished out there." Judging from his tone, Neil wasn't placated.

Lacey sighed. "I guess I'd better start dinner. You're welcome to stay." Then a slight, grudging smile curved her mouth. "Of course, you're also welcome to hang around afterward and help clean up this mess."

She headed for the kitchen without waiting for an answer, but came to an abrupt halt in the doorway, an expression of horror on her face. Her kitchen! Her beautiful, spotlessly clean kitchen! It looked as if one of those cookware parties had been held in it, only whoever had done the cooking obviously hadn't seen fit to clean up after himself.

"Now don't blow your stack," Neil muttered behind her, and Lacey whirled on him.

"Out! Out of this house, before you destroy what's left of it," she ordered furiously.

"I meant to wash up, but we started a game of Chutes and Ladders, and I just—"

"*Out!* Before I throw one of those filthy pans at you! How could *anybody* dirty half a dozen pans and three skillets fixing soup and sandwiches!" she railed in angry disbelief.

"Some of it's from breakfast," Neil admitted guiltily, then backed out the door when she reached for the handle of a ten-inch skillet encrusted with burned cheese. "All right, I'm going! Maybe you'll have calmed down by tomorrow morning."

She had, but a visit home at lunchtime to supervise his culinary efforts found the three of them sitting at the table wolfing down double-decker cheeseburgers, French fries and large Cokes from the take-home window of a fast-food restaurant. Lacey's mouth went tight as she picked up the grease-soaked waxed paper container for an order of fries.

"I don't feed my children junk food," she said tersely.

Neil's mouth formed as thin a line as hers as he came off his stool and took hold of her elbow to half drag her out of the dinette and down the hall. The twins looked on curiously and kept munching at their burgers.

"There's just no satisfying you, is there?" he snarled when they reached the entry. "Yesterday you flew into a rage because the kitchen was a little messy—"

"A little messy!" Lacey choked.

"So today I *bought* lunch rather than risk dirtying up your precious kitchen, and now you're harping about that! Since when are hamburgers junk food, I'd like to know!"

"The hamburgers *I* make are not junk food," Lacey informed him haughtily. "Because I know exactly what's in them. Can you say the same about those things *you're* feeding them? And those French fries are swimming in grease, which is loaded with cholesterol, not to mention the soft drinks! I know you can afford an enormous bill for dental work, but I'd like to see them keep their teeth as long as possible!"

"Their teeth aren't all going to drop out of their heads from drinking a couple of Cokes, are they? And as for junk food, I didn't hear you complaining about your pal Mussolini buying them pizza!" Neil accused.

"For your information that was the one and only

time he's ever brought food into this house!" Lacey stormed back at him.

"A freeloader, huh? I should've guessed."

"Look here, Neil," Lacey ground out furiously. "Paul knew I'd be working late that night, and he was trying to help out, that's all." She added tersely, "He realizes how difficult it is to be both mother and breadwinner at the same time, and he was trying to make things a little easier for me!"

"Well, what the hell do you think *I'm* doing here?" Neil demanded loudly.

"Keep your voice down!" she shouted back at him. "If filling them full of sugar, cholesterol and Lord knows what kind of chemical additives is your idea of helping, I think they might be better off on their own! Diet is very important during a child's formative years, and I won't have you wrecking their health just to save yourself a little work."

"Wrecking their health!" Neil echoed in disbelief. "Lacey, you're positively paranoid about this health business. You're blowing this whole thing completely out of proportion. You sound like one of those nuts who go around eating roots and berries and look like walking scarecrows."

Lacey's cheeks flamed because she suspected he was at least partly right. She probably *was* overreacting, but she persisted out of sheer stubbornness more than anything else.

"Thank you very much," she retorted. "I guess you'd rather I didn't care, and fed my children the kind of nutritionally empty junk most kids eat today? Sugar and cholesterol have a cumulative effect,

Neil, in case you didn't know. I guess it wouldn't bother you at all if one or both of them dropped dead of a heart attack before he even reached middle age?"

He blanched, and a thin ring of tension appeared around his compressed lips. "That's a rotten thing to say," he rasped.

He turned away abruptly, and the intensity of his reaction shamed Lacey enough to cool her temper.

"I know it was," she admitted. "I'm sorry, Neil." Then she sighed heavily. "This just isn't going to work. Every time we're together, we argue. We don't seem to agree on anything anymore. I guess we've just both changed too much."

Neil spun back around, his anger revived. "Don't be ridiculous!" he snapped impatiently. "You think other married couples don't fight? That's part of being married—you fight, and then you make up." His sudden grin took her by surprise. "We've got the fighting part down pat. Now all we need to work on is the making up."

Lacey shook her head doubtfully, but she couldn't completely repress the tiny smile that tugged at the corners of her mouth.

Wednesday's fight was much less heated and shorter in duration. It started when Lacey arrived home to find that Neil had gone out and bought a home video-game system and then hooked it up to her television. He and Scott were taking turns blasting away at a horde of space creatures before they could land and conquer the earth, while Todd waited patiently to play the winner.

"I thought you weren't going to spoil them with expensive presents," she observed as she came up behind him.

Neil didn't turn around; he was too busy trying to avoid destruction by the invading aliens. "It's only one present, and it's supposed to be educational," he murmured absently. Apparently answering wrecked his concentration, because the next instant his laser cannon disappeared from the screen with the same sound an overripe watermelon would make hitting the pavement, and he muttered a disgusted oath.

"*Neil!*"

Scott looked up with a grin. "It's okay, mom. He always says that when he gets zapped."

"Oh, he does, does he?" Lacey asked as she glowered at Neil. He unfolded himself and came off the floor with a shrug and an unrepentant grin.

"Take it easy. They haven't started to repeat it."

"We'd get our mouths washed out, that's why," Todd remarked soberly as he moved up to take his father's place.

Lacey clapped a hand over her mouth to contain a burst of laughter, and then Neil was pushing her out the door and up the stairs. Her shoulders shook under his hands, and when she stopped and turned she saw that he was barely containing his amusement, as well. His arms came around her, and she collapsed against him in helpless, silent laughter.

"I ought to wash your mouth out, too," she gasped as tears ran down her cheeks. "You're absolutely impossible."

Neil leaned back to wipe the tears away with cool fingers. He was smiling in a way she'd never seen him smile before: like a man who has everything he's ever wanted in the world and can't believe his good luck.

"I know," he chuckled. "Thank goodness I'm so lovable, too. Listen, why don't we all go out for dinner. My treat."

Lacey smiled back as she looped her arms around his neck. "I've got a better idea. Why don't we have a pizza delivered, with every kind of junk we can get on it."

"All *right!*" Neil said softly. His eyes glowed as he bent his head, and Lacey met him halfway, without the slightest hesitation.

"They're not fighting, they're just kissing," a disappointed voice said from the bottom of the stairs, and Neil lifted his head with a mock groan.

"Give me a break, you guys," he complained. "How am I supposed to soften her up with you heckling from the sidelines?"

There were muffled giggles from downstairs, and then the electronic blips resumed as the twins went back to their game.

"Is that what you call this—softening me up?" Lacey asked as she kissed the slight indentation in his chin.

"Mmm, they're supposed to be helping, but lately I've had the feeling we were fighting a lost cause," Neil drawled.

"So the three of you have been conspiring against me," she murmured as she stretched to lazily run her tongue around the outside of his ear.

"Are you mad?" Neil asked humorously. He bent his head to give her freer access to his neck and ear, and Lacey felt his quickened breathing against her skin. It suddenly occurred to her that she was flirting with him, something she thought she'd forgotten how to do.

"No," she answered in a throaty purr, then gently captured his earlobe between her teeth. "What I am is hungry."

Neil groaned as he hauled her up against him and mouthed the side of her neck. "Me too," he admitted huskily.

"I meant for pizza." The breathless quality of her voice ruined the light effect Lacey was trying for, and she suddenly had to fight against dizzying waves of weakness.

"*I* meant for you," Neil whispered in her ear, and then his mouth was on hers, hot and urgent as his hands pressed her to him, forcing her to acknowledge his desire.

His kiss was devastating but all too brief before he tore his mouth away with a smothered moan. "But I'll settle for pizza, if I have to," he murmured as he released her.

There was no way Lacey could answer the not-so-subtle question in that remark; his smoldering gaze was too knowing, too sexually aware. She escaped with the excuse of phoning in their order, and her hands shook as she looked up the number for the Pizza Palace in the directory.

Paul had been right: Neil's patience wasn't unlimited, and from the way he'd just held her and kissed her, she knew it was fast running out. Any day now he would demand to know her decision; and if she made the one they both knew she was headed for, he would expect to resume their marriage with all the rights he'd enjoyed before, including the unqualified right to make love to her.

While he'd been gentle and patiently tender so far, she remembered all too well how wildly abandoned he could be at times, and it was that thought that troubled her. If she agreed to be truly his wife again, she couldn't expect him to exercise restraint indefinitely, and yet it was his loss of control she feared most. She knew it was cowardly to place all the responsibility for self-control with Neil, but the memories of that last night were still too strong whenever he held her, and she could feel the latent strength in his body.

She was subdued and quiet the rest of the evening, and Neil seemed to sense her mood. He gave his attention to his sons until they were tucked in for the night and he and Lacey had returned to the family room to clear away the plates, napkins and glasses. When the dishwasher was loaded he reached out to turn her toward him. His expression was solemn, his eyes hooded and unreadable.

"You know your time's running out, don't you?" he asked softly, one hand cupping the curve of her jaw.

Lacey nodded wordlessly. As Neil gazed down into her eyes, he sighed softly.

"You're just one big mass of anxieties, aren't you? I guess it wouldn't do any good to tell you you're borrowing trouble—that it won't be the catastrophe you think?"

"We can't know that until it happens, though, can we?"

"I know that I want you. And I know that you want me, but that you're still afraid," he said, his tone grave. "I *don't* know what else I can do to reassure you, to make you believe me when I say I'd rather die than hurt you again." He took an impatient breath when his voice roughened and grew harsh, then went on more calmly. "You're just going to have to take me on faith, Lacey. When you get right down to it, that's what marriage is all about—faith and trust. Either you trust me, or you don't."

"I trusted you once before," she replied without thinking, and regretted it at once when anger flared in Neil's eyes, and his hand dropped away from her like a rock.

"I won't have you throwing that in my face for the rest of our lives," he said in a flat, hard tone.

"I didn't mean to. I'm sorry." Lacey made a futile gesture with her hands. "It's just been on my mind tonight."

He moved angrily away, then turned back to face her. "The only way you're going to get it *out* of your mind is to put the past behind you and start concentrating on the future," he told her. "And we both know what the first step is, Lacey."

When she didn't respond he looked at her for a long moment.

"This has gone far enough," he announced suddenly. "I heard from Bob today. He'll be here late tomorrow morning. Since I'll probably be busy with him most of the day, that gives you until Friday to make up your mind one way or the other. After Friday I'll make it up *for* you."

It was a threat, and Lacey's eyes registered it as such; but Neil didn't relent as she stared at him in anxious appeal.

"Don't worry about the boys," he told her curtly as he turned for the door. "They won't be in the way tomorrow. We'll just carry on as usual."

Lacey didn't get much sleep that night, and the next morning she had to use a cover stick to mask the dark circles under her eyes. Wonderful, she thought, grimacing at her reflection in the mirror; at this rate she'd soon look older than Neil. She certainly felt it this morning.

It was after seven-thirty when his truck pulled into the drive. *Cutting it close*, Lacey thought resentfully, *probably on purpose*. She barely said two words to him, hurriedly kissing the boys goodbye and grabbing her purse on the way out.

"Wait a minute." Neil followed her outside, but she just kept walking.

"I can't. Thanks to you, I'm already running late."

When she reached for the car door, his hand was there first. She lifted her head and gave him a withering look.

"Making another power play, are we?" she said in a flat, hard voice. "Flexing our muscles again, proving who's boss, who calls the shots? Get away from my car, Neil."

Neil's mouth turned down at the corners, but he didn't remove his hand. "I was hoping I could convince you to take the day off and spend it with Bob and the boys and me."

Lacey expelled an exasperated breath. "Just like that? Just don't show up at the office today? Whatever happened to 'I realize how much your independence means to you'? What do you think I do all day, Neil, sit behind a desk and file my nails?" She all but shouted the last sentence, so angry she could have kicked him.

For a moment she thought he was about to shout back at her, or maybe vent his own anger in an even more demonstrative way. She tensed, ready to lash out at him if he so much as leaned in her direction, but he only exhaled a disgusted sigh and removed his hand from the car door.

"You're determined to fight me every inch of the way, aren't you?" he said. "I can't open my mouth without you twisting whatever I say, misinterpreting everything so that I always come out the villain. You're always so defensive with me!"

"How can you expect me to be anything else, when you're constantly pressuring me, issuing ultimatums and setting deadlines," Lacey countered.

He winced at that, but recovered quickly to demand, "Well, what do you expect me to do—just sit around twiddling my thumbs until you come up with the guts to make some kind of commitment?"

"You promised to give me time," she reminded him tersely.

"And I have! Time enough, and then some. Look, Lacey, you're no coward, so stop acting like one! You know good and well I'm not going to hurt you again. You've known it for weeks!"

She gazed at him steadily, trying not to let him see how that last remark had unnerved her, catching her off balance and stunning her with its simple inarguable truth.

Pride and pure obstinacy made her retort in a throaty murmur, "There are different ways of hurting people, Neil."

His jaw clenched, and too late she saw that she'd pushed him past impatience into real anger.

"You really know how to push me to the limit," he muttered furiously. "The 'ultimatum' *and* the deadline still stand, Mrs. Hartmann. You've got until tomorrow morning to come up with the answer I want, and you can bet your last dollar I'll be here bright and early." And then he turned on his heel and strode back to the house, like a man who knew exactly where he was going and what he'd find when he got there.

"HONESTLY, LACEY, you're as twitchy as a long-tailed cat in a room full of rocking chairs," Ellen remarked in amusement. Vi had gone to the post office, and the two of them were alone. "You keep hopping up and down, forgetting where you've put things, and you jump a foot every time the phone rings. Wouldn't have anything to do with that gorgeous husband of yours, would it?" she asked with a shrewd gleam in her eye.

Lacey's mouth pulled down at the corners. "It's got everything to do with him."

Ellen nodded sagely. "Putting on the pressure, is he? Doesn't surprise me. I figured once he got to know those two little darlings, he'd want to be more than just a part-time daddy. So what's the problem? The two of you still fighting?''

"No," Lacey admitted reluctantly. "But he's started laying down terms and conditions." Her mouth twisted wryly. "I've got until tomorrow to decide to give marriage another try, or he'll decide for me."

To her consternation, Ellen chuckled. "I told you the first time I heard his voice he was the take-charge type, didn't I? Personally I think you've got to be nuts for holding out this long. Well, speak of the devil," she murmured as she glanced through the front window and caught sight of Neil approaching. "Mm-mmm, *I* sure wouldn't mind waking up to that every morning."

Lacey frowned at the older woman's teasing, but she couldn't deny the almost electrical charge that swept through her at the sight of him. He'd discarded the jeans—probably in honor of Bob Anderson's visit—in favor of tailored navy slacks and a light-weight pale blue velour pullover with a V neck. For the couple of seconds he stood in front of the plate-glass door before opening it Lacey had a full view of his tall virile form, and her stomach did somersaults while her pulse began to race crazily.

The she realized he wasn't alone. He stood aside, and their sons half ran, half skipped past him into the office, followed by a middle-aged man in a business suit.

"Hi, mom."

"Hi, Ellen."

After the perfunctory greetings, the boys headed straight for the calculator on Ellen's desk. Lacey looked around to see Bob advancing on her, his face wreathed in a huge smile.

"Lacey! It's not possible! You're even more beautiful than ever." And then he was hugging her enthusiastically while she laughed over his shoulder.

"You always were an old flatterer, Bob. It's good to see you," she said sincerely. "How are Martha and the girls?" Bob and his wife had two daughters who would both be in their late teens.

"Fine, just fine," he answered proudly. "Marcie and Susan are turning into real beauties, just like their mother. But those two of yours!" He shook his head as he glanced at the twins. "You could've knocked me over with a feather when I got here and found Neil out at that farm with two little Neils in tow. I can't get over how much like him they look."

Lacey's gaze shifted to Neil. "They're certainly their father's sons, all right." Her voice came out sounding a little husky. From the gleam in his eye, she thought for a moment Neil would cross the four feet or so separating them and do something guaranteed to embarrass her, but he only smiled benignly.

"We came to invite you to a cookout tonight," Neil said smoothly. "Out at the farm. The terrible two are in charge of the menu, and you don't have to bring anything but yourself."

"A cookout?" Lacey repeated in surprise.

"Yeah, mom, it'll be neat," Scott claimed enthusiastically.

"And we're gonna camp out after we eat," Todd put in. "We already took the tent out there this morning, and our sleeping bags. Yours, too," he tacked on with a grin.

Lacey's eyes flew back to Neil. He lifted one brow in mocking challenge, knowing she wasn't likely to dispute his plans in front of both Ellen and Bob. His arrogance angered her. If he thought she was going to spend the night in a tent with him—even with the boys for chaperons—he was mistaken.

While she was introducing Bob and Ellen, Neil rounded up his sons and herded them out. They'd barely had time to make it to his truck before the horn tooted impatiently. Bob glanced toward the door with a chuckle.

"Sounds like I'm being summoned. I've been invited to stay and share hamburgers and hot dogs with the Hartmann clan tonight, so we can have a nice long visit then, Lacey."

That parting remark stayed with her all afternoon. If anyone would know what had happened during the past eight years to change Neil so drastically, Bob would. Maybe during that nice long visit, he could satisfy her curiosity.

All afternoon Lacey was aware of the tension building in her, growing steadily, despite her efforts to concentrate on work. And there was plenty of that! Thank goodness Rick only had a week of school left, and both Joyce and Marion would be back from vacation on the weekend. Even part-time help was better than no help at all. It was just her rotten luck that Neil had come back into her life when she was being run practically off her feet. No wonder he'd come on so strong about her not spending enough time with the boys—from what he'd seen so far, it must appear that she was never home, never shared any quality time with them.

She sighed as she pushed a file drawer closed. Well, starting next week things should begin to lighten up, and he'd be able to gain a different perspective on her life-style. Normally, when she wasn't working herself half to death, she and the boys did a lot of fun things together. They also spent a lot of time just goofing off and enjoying one another. And now, she realized with a feeling of pleased anticipation, Neil would be here to join them. They could do all the things families were supposed to do together— go to Saturday matinees, take long walks after supper, play Monopoly, or just sit around watching TV and munching popcorn in the evenings.

When she realized the direction her thoughts were taking, she also realized the decision he wanted from her had already been made. Not consciously, perhaps, but her subconscious had been busily carrying on its own rebellion all along, wearing away at her stubborn resistance, eroding the residual bitterness and antagonism, until all that was left was a sort of wary acceptance. She would live with him as his wife—assuming all the duties and responsibilities the title implied—and she would tell him so tonight.

The decision made, her tension should have eased, but perversely did not. It only altered her mood from anger at his chauvinistic arrogance to what she had to admit was her sexual anxiety. Neil had never been blessed with a wealth of patience, and once she'd capitulated she didn't expect for one moment that he would be prepared to give her any more time. The way he saw it, she'd taken eight years too long already.

After work she went home to change into a pair of cutoffs and a halter top. She hardly thought a cook-out on a farm in the middle of the boondocks called for formal dress, and it was too hot for jeans. The boys were waiting to meet her, each taking a hand to pull her around to the back of the house.

"Dad's firin' up the grill," Todd informed her, and she smiled as she imagined Neil drawling the words his son had parroted in a juvenile version of his deep, slow voice.

"But we get to do the real cooking," Scott pointed out importantly. "We even got marshmallows to roast on sticks."

Neil was just putting a match to the charcoal as they came around the corner of the house. Fortunately the twins released her hands to run forward, because Lacey stopped dead in her tracks at the sight of him.

He, too, was wearing cutoffs—would wonders never cease—and no shirt. All the blood seemed to rush to Lacey's head, and for a moment she felt dizzy. It had been a long time since she had seen so much of Neil exposed, and the sight of his long muscular legs and broad tapered back did unexpected things to her pulse and respiration. When he heard the boys he glanced over his shoulder, then casually reached for a short-sleeved cotton shirt draped over a lawn chair at his side. He half turned to put it on and button it part way up his chest, then faced her with a lazy smile as he tucked in the tail and came to where she was standing, as if planted there.

"Caught in the act. The management of this place requires patrons to wear a shirt and shoes." Then, as he appreciatively eyed her skimpy halter top, he added, "I'd say you just barely meet the requirement. Not that I'm complaining, mind you."

The light in his eyes made Lacey feel flustered and foolishly embarrassed. He'd seen her in much less, after all. Before she could think of a flip retort, Todd asked his father if he was going to give her the tour now.

"You bet." Neil's wide grin told Lacey he was perfectly aware of her discomfort and the reason for it. "You guys stay out here and babysit Mr. Anderson, okay?"

The boys giggled, and Bob smiled from the chaise lounge he occupied in the shade of a huge pin oak.

"Don't worry about me. If I go to sleep, wake me when it's time to roast the marshmallows."

"The tour begins here," Neil drawled as he led the way to the back door and opened it for her to pass through.

Lacey stepped inside, slightly skeptical that enough could have been done to the house in two short weeks to merit a tour, then came to a halt two feet inside the kitchen.

"Neil!"

He ignored both her startled exclamation and the amazement in her voice as he placed both hands on her shoulders to turn her in a slow circle.

"A firm of kitchen designers from Marion did it. They just finished today. What do you think?"

She couldn't find words to tell him for a minute or two. If she hadn't known better, she'd have sworn she was in a different house from the one he'd bought. The entire kitchen had been remodeled and reequipped with the most up-to-the-minute fixtures available. There was even an indoor barbecue, with a huge copper vent hood suspended above it. The center work island itself must have been at least six feet long, with its own sink and a trash compactor built into the cabinet below it.

"It's...oh, Neil, it's beautiful! But, it must have cost the earth!" She turned to face him with a troubled frown. "I hope you didn't do all this with me in mind."

"You!" he scoffed. "I did it with *me* in mind. Neil Hartmann, househusband, remember?" Then, before she could dwell on the possibilities inherent in that remark, he clasped her hand and started pulling her after him. "Come on, there are nine more rooms on the tour."

As he guided her through the downstairs, Lacey's amazement grew. The smells of sawdust, turpentine and fresh paint lingered in the air. Walls had already been relocated or removed completely to open up the existing space and put it to more efficient use, and from the inside she noticed that all or at least most of the windows had been replaced. How on earth had the workmen managed to do so much in such a short time.? *It must be costing him a fortune in overtime*, she thought as he started leading her up the stairs.

"I let the boys decide whether they wanted separate rooms or not," he said as he paused outside the first door on the right. His mouth slanted in amusement. "The vote was unanimous for a single room, but they wanted more space than they've got in your house."

He threw open the door and pulled her inside, and Lacey sucked in her breath at the sheer dimensions of the room.

"You tore down the whole wall!" she exclaimed.

"It's all right. It wasn't a load-bearing wall," Neil told her. "This way, they've got one end for sleeping and studying, and the other end for a playroom. Then, when they get older, if they decide they want more privacy we can divide the space into two rooms again. They picked out the paper and paint, by the way."

Lacey's eyes traveled slowly from one end of the enormous room to the other and back again, and she shook her head in wonder. It was about forty feet long and twenty-five feet wide. The bedroom end was painted a soft blue-gray shade with white woodwork, and the playroom end had dark blue wainscoting with *Star Wars* patterned wallpaper on the upper half of the walls.

"They never said a word about any of this," she murmured in dazed surprise.

"Of course not. It was a conspiracy, remember? Come on, there's one more stop on the tour."

He pointed out that there were two more bedrooms across the hall which hadn't been renovated yet, but they passed them without stopping, headed for a door Lacey knew opened onto a large attic area above the kitchen. Her curiosity was aroused. What on earth could he have done with that dark, dismal space?

"I saved the best for last," Neil said, his hand resting on the new brass knob of the freshly varnished hardwood door. An odd, almost hopeful look flickered in his eyes as the knob turned under his hand, and then he murmured, "*Voilà—the pièce de résistance*," as the door swung silently open on new brass hinges.

Lacey's breath caught. She wasn't even aware of Neil's hand on the small of her back, gently urging her inside. Sunlight streamed through the newly installed dormer windows on either side of the room. No, that wasn't right—it was more than one room. Even though the six-foot-wide doorframes now stood empty, she could see that partitioning walls had been built to divide the space into three separate areas.

"Master bedroom at the far end, dressing area and bath in the middle, and a combination office-study at this end," Neil supplied softly at her back.

Lacey's gaze traveled the length of the former attic, and she picked out the same tint of blue she'd seen in his hair, on the walls of the bedroom and dressing area. In the study end, where they were standing, the primed wallboard absorbed the rays of the late afternoon sun so that the whole area seemed to glow with golden light.

"I'd never have believed you could have done this," she told him in awe. "This...suite—that's the only word to do it justice—and the boys' room and that kitchen! Neil, it's all incredible, and all in two weeks!"

One of his arms circled her waist to pull her back against him. "And I've got the blisters and smashed thumbs to prove what a job it was, too," he pointed out.

Lacey started, jerking against him. "You . . . !"

"Me," he asserted with a touch of pride. "Oh, I won't claim I didn't have plenty of help, but I wanted to be able to say this was *my* house, that I'd invested more than just my hard-earned capital in it."

His mocking reminder of her words the day he gave her the check for the farm brought quick color to Lacey's cheeks. But she had been judging him by past performance, after all, relying on knowledge of him that was no longer valid.

Neil's other arm came around her as he bent to lay his cheek alongside hers. "Have I proved myself yet?" he asked tenderly. Then, before she could answer, he seemed to switch subjects. "You know, this study area could be used as a bedroom, instead, if the lady of the house felt she needed the security of her own room."

His deep voice was close to her ear, his warm breath fanning her cheek. Something inside Lacey seemed to crack. She almost felt a fissure appear in what remained of the protective shell she had built up around her heart over the years. Her head fell back to rest on Neil's shoulder, and his hold tightened fractionally in immediate response. He was waiting for her to say something, to acknowledge the offer he'd made. His whole body was tensed against her back.

"*If*—" she stressed the word faintly "—there was a lady of the house, I'm sure she'd much rather share a room . . . and a bed—" her voice faltered only slightly "—with the gentleman of the house."

The last word had barely passed her lips before she was turned swiftly, roughly, in his arms. His mouth was hard, seeking hers urgently as his hands clasped her to him. Under seige, the crack widened, and a warmth streamed through it to suffuse every part of her. Lacey was acutely, intensely aware of his hair-roughed legs as he wedged one knee between hers. The last shattered pieces of the shell disintegrated in the heat of her passion, which now equalled Neil's. Her hands sought and found the opening of his shirt and shoved it aside, her fingers busily renewing their acquaintance with his warm, heavily matted chest. When he left her mouth for her throat Lacey moaned softly in protest.

"I know I gave you until tomorrow, and I heard that big 'if,'" he murmured hoarsely as his hand wandered down her back to press her even closer, "but you can't stop me from feeling encouraged."

Hardly hearing him for the pounding in her ears, Lacey pushed against him in a blatantly sexual plea for fulfillment as she turned her head to blindly seek his mouth again.

"Oh, Lacey!" The strain he was under showed as his grip tightened convulsively, and he gave in to temptation long enough to brand her lips in a hard, possessive kiss before dragging his mouth away. "The first piece of furniture I move in here is a king-size bed," he growled against the side of her neck.

"I wish it was here now," Lacey admitted

breathlessly. "Oh, Neil, I want you. It's been so long."

The breath rushed from him and he shuddered violently, his arms nearly cracking her ribs in the fierceness of his response. Under her cheek his heart was racing out of control, but it beat no harder or faster than her own as one of her hands forced its way between their bodies to grasp him in an aggressive display of her very basic needs.

Fast losing his control, Neil suddenly twisted, clamping his hand over hers to press it hard against him; but then he was forcefully putting her from him, his breathing labored as he struggled to restrain himself.

"Come on," he said harshly as he took hold of her hand. "If we stay up here we'll both end up with splinters from the floorboards."

He held Lacey close to his side, his hand curved to fit her hip as they started down the hall. When they reached the stairs he murmured, "The kids can have the tent tonight. We'll drag our sleeping bags out under the stars."

He didn't look at her, and he hadn't phrased it as a question. Nevertheless, Lacey leaned her cheek against his chest, and her arm hugged his lean waist in silent agreement.

Once Neil and Lacey were outside again, the boys claimed Neil's attention for help with cooking the hamburgers and hot dogs, and he released her with obvious reluctance. Lacey carried a folding lawn chair over to sit beside Bob, who was watching the threesome with a smile.

"He's like a different man," he remarked quietly.

This was her chance, Lacey realized, but instinct warned her to go slowly and cautiously. Bob was fiercely loyal to Neil, and if he suspected she was fishing for information, he would probably turn into the proverbial clam.

"Yes," she nodded. "I never would have believed he'd be such a wonderful father. He never seems to run out of patience with them," she added.

"True, the old Neil Hartmann was notably lacking in patience and tolerance," Bob said, "but then after what he's been through, it's no wonder he's mellowed a little."

Lacey conquered the impulse to ask outright what he meant by that. *Slowly*, she reminded herself, *go slowly*.

"He looks so much better than when he first came here," she remarked thoughtfully. "He was so pale, and he looked exhausted. Now he's as brown and fit as the boys, and did he tell you he's been doing a lot of the work on the house himself?"

Bob nodded, his smile disappearing as a vaguely troubled look came into his eyes. "He did, and I told him I wasn't sure it was such a good idea. I know the doctors encouraged him to exercise, but I'm afraid he might be overdoing it. You know Neil—he never does anything halfway."

He glanced at Lacey, and when he saw how the color had left her face he was immediately contrite.

"Uh, oh. I've put my foot in it, haven't I? I didn't mean to worry you, Lacey. I'm sure Neil knows his own capabilities better than anyone else. And with you around to keep an eye on him—well, a woman has ways of persuading her man to see reason that a doctor can't use," he added with a grin.

A numbing cold had begun to steal over her, and her heart thudded heavily in her chest.

"I didn't know," she said huskily. "Are you saying he shouldn't exert himself at all?"

"Oh, no! No," Bob repeated with a firm shake of his head. "Like I said, the doctors encouraged him to exercise, to build up his stamina again, but gradually. After all," he added with a grim glance toward Neil, "his heart stopped completely during that stomach surgery, and then he had that episode of fibrillation while he was still in recovery. Scared the hell out of me, I don't mind telling you. I was there when they slapped those paddles on his chest and sent that charge of electricity through him, and that's something I hope I never have to witness again."

9

LACEY FELT light-headed. She was thankful she was already sitting down, because she knew her legs wouldn't have supported her at that moment. Bob turned to her again, coming upright on the chaise and leaning forward in anxious concern when he noticed her shallow breathing and the stricken look in her eyes.

"Good Lord," he muttered in sudden realization. "You didn't know about any of that, did you?"

Lacey shook her head numbly. She closed her eyes and tried to force her chaotic thoughts into some kind or order. "Stomach surgery, you said," she whispered. "What kind of stomach surgery?"

Bob hesitated, then apparently decided he'd already said too much to avoid answering. "He had a perforated ulcer. That means—"

"I know what it means," Lacey interrupted in a trembling voice. "Was it emergency surgery, or did his doctor have it scheduled ahead of time?"

Bob snorted. "Emergency, of course. He developed the first ulcer about seven or eight years ago, right after the two of you split." He gave her a sharp, sympathetic look. "I don't know the whole story, but I always assumed it had something to do with Jason

Trent and the ridiculous accusations he made to try
and save his own hide. Anyway—" Bob's voice became brisk again, "—true to form, Neil ignored all
the advice about diet and cutting back on his work
load. If anything, he worked harder than ever after
you were gone. It was like the company was all he
had left, the only reason he had to keep going. Then
one day about nine months ago he started hemor-
rhaging during a staff meeting. We rushed him to the
hospital, and they decided to operate immediately.
Apparently he'd been bleeding internally for some
time but didn't even tell his own doctor about the
symptoms." Bob shook his head slowly, his eyes sad.
"It was almost as if he had some kind of death wish,"
he said under his breath.

He was looking at Neil again, and Lacey's stunned
gaze followed his. It was hard to believe the man so
obviously enjoying his sons as they poked and
prodded at hot dogs had come within a hair's
breadth of dying such a short time ago. A sudden
chill raised goose bumps on her arms, though even
under the shade of the oak tree it was unseasonably
warm for late June. She had a sudden, vivid mental
image of Neil lying in a hospital bed, tubes and
needles invading his body and electronic monitors
linking him to ugly machines as he fought for his
life. Bob's words about paddles and electric shocks
returned to torture her imagination with another
picture even more horrifying and she squeezed her
eyes shut.

"Lacey?" Bob's anxious voice came to her from far
away. She opened her eyes to find him sitting side-

ways on the chaise, bent toward her in an attitude of concern.

"He didn't tell me," she whispered. "He deliberately kept it from me."

"He didn't want you to worry," Bob explained kindly, and Lacey shook her head in denial.

"No. It was more than that." There was a quiet certainty in her voice as her gaze returned to Neil.

Bob looked puzzled, but his voice was heavy with regret. "He'll have my hide for telling you."

"Don't worry," Lacey murmured. "I won't let on that I know until after you're gone."

She remembered what Neil had said about spreading their sleeping bags under the stars tonight, and just as vividly remembered the furious pounding of his heart when desire had flared between them upstairs. He hadn't told her because he knew she would fear for his health, and was afraid she wouldn't be able to overcome it enough to let him make love to her again. With a sinking heart, Lacey admitted to herself that he was probably right.

Bob left shortly after seven, while there was still more than an hour of daylight left. The boys waved goodbye, then disappeared behind the house to work on their garden. Bob embraced Lacey affectionately when she and Neil walked him to his car, his eyes giving a reassurance he didn't dare speak aloud. Lacey permitted Neil's arm to remain around her waist until the rented car had pulled from the gravel lane onto the road beyond, and then she pried his hand away and walked out of his loose embrace toward the house.

Neil frowned at her withdrawal. "Having second thoughts?" he asked quietly as they entered the kitchen. He settled into a white pine captain's chair, extending a hand to Lacey to draw her onto his lap.

"Not the way you mean," Lacey finally answered. Meeting his eyes, she instructed "Unbutton your shirt."

Neil's eyes started to warm with anticipation and his hand lifted, but then his expression suddenly froze as a wary look crept into them. "What have you got in mind?" he drawled, his fingers hesitating over the fourth button down from his neck.

"Maybe I just want to look at you." Lacey's voice was husky, but not for the reason he might have thought. When his hand remained still, she reached for the button herself. Neil stopped her, his fingers curling around hers.

"Lacey," he began, "There's something—" He stopped abruptly, his eyes narrowing at her closed, almost hostile expression. "What is it?" he asked tersely. "You've been moody ever since we went back outside, when you sat down next to Bob—" He broke off, his eyes kindling with suspicion.

"Don't stop now," Lacey said. "What's the matter, are you beginning to realize that good old Bob might have given away some of your secrets?" Her voice had gone hard in anger. "Take off your shirt, Neil. Let me see the scar. I want to see for myself what they did to you."

"That big blabbermouth!" he exploded. "I might have known he couldn't keep his trap shut! Listen, Lacey—"

"I want to see," she persisted, her voice low and throaty. "Is it so bad you have to hide it from me, is that it? Now I know why you were in such a hurry to put your shirt on when I got here. You should have told me!" She cried the last in a shaken voice, jerking her hand from his grasp.

Neil rose and put his hands on both sides of her face, framing it gently as he noticed the moisture shimmering on her lashes.

"It's not that bad," he said softly. "And I didn't tell you because I was afraid you'd overreact, that's all."

Lacey wasn't to be deterred. "If it's not that bad, then let me see," she insisted.

Neil hesitated for a moment, and then he quickly unfastened his shirt, his gaze never leaving her face.

"There. See—all healed," he said briskly. He started to pull the shirt together again, but Lacey stopped him, her fingers trembling as they traced the neat, hard ridge of white scar tissue on his flat brown stomach.

"Oh, Neil," she whispered in a voice that quavered and nearly broke.

"No." He took her hands away and put her arms around his waist, pulling her close to his chest. "Don't, baby. It's all right. That pesky little devil and the two others are completely healed. Listen, if you need proof, I helped demolish a large deluxe pizza just last night, remember?"

"Oh, no!" Lacey's low, husky voice held dread. "With Italian sausage and pepperoni...."

"And anchovies and extra peppers, the way you

like," he added lightly. "And I didn't even need an Alka Seltzer. Satisfied?"

She relaxed a little in his arms, then stiffened in anger. "You have to be insane to have eaten all that in the first place!" she accused, lifting her head to glare at him.

"And if I'd said, 'Sorry, darling, but since they sliced away half my stomach I don't tolerate spicy foods very well,' how would you have reacted?" Neil queried her gently.

Lacey's eyes glazed with horror, and she jerked against him reflexively.

"Teasing!" Neil claimed when he saw how the thoughtless words had affected her. "Lacey, I was only teasing! Do you have to dramatize everything?"

"Me!" she choked, still not recovered from the shock of what he'd said.

"All right," he relented with a sigh. "I could have phrased that a little more tactfully. But my point is, I couldn't have refused to eat the pizza without making you suspicious, and as it turned out, it didn't even give me a twinge of discomfort anyway. Now, will you promise not to worry?" He smiled down at her, his eyes soft and warm as his hands exerted gentle pressure on her back. "I promise, sweetheart," he murmured huskily, "that scar over my breadbasket won't hinder me in any way when I make love to you. And I want to. Oh, how I want to. I'm starved for you, darling."

His lips coaxed hers to part, and then his tongue invaded her mouth, hard yet gentle in its slow, tantalizing exploration. Lacey's fingers clutched the back of his shirt as she fought for sanity. There was something she needed to remember, something important, some reason she mustn't let him do this. But whatever the reason was, her brain refused to call it forth. Unaware of what she was doing, she pulled at his shirt until it was hanging from his arms, held on him only because they were wrapped so tightly around her.

Moving into the living room as if in a trance, they collapsed onto the soft divan, where Neil murmured, "There, that's better," as his hand slid around her back and his fingers found their way under the edge of her halter.

"Touch me, Lacey," he asked, his voice rough with urgency. "Don't hold back any longer. Please, darling."

Her eager hands were only too willing to accede to his wishes. They reveled in the solid warmth of his lean back beneath her palms, rejoiced at the involuntary flex of his muscles. His strength was no longer something to fear, but a wonderfully integral part of his masculinity, both a contrast and a complement to her femininity.

It wasn't until her hands strayed to his furry chest and felt the disturbed beating of his heart that memory—and with it fear—returned. She pulled out of his arms, her eyes wide with awareness, and jumped up.

"Lacey!" Neil started to reach for her, then stopped himself with an obvious effort. "I thought we'd gotten past that—that you weren't afraid of me anymore," he said in regret.

Lacey's head jerked in denial. "I'm not." Her voice was tight and strained, her breathing shallow.

Neil's brow furrowed in confusion. "Then what is it? You *are* afraid—I can feel it, see it in your eyes."

She tried to swallow and found that her mouth and throat were too dry. Fear was a cold vise inside her. "It's your heart," she managed in a feeble whisper.

Neil stared at her, his expression blank and uncomprehending for a moment. "My heart?" he echoed in bewilderment, and then understanding dawned and his eyes glinted with anger. "My heart," he repeated in disgust. "Damn! Bob didn't waste any time filling you in on my entire medical history, did he?" He swore again, more forcefully. "Lacey—" he rose, taking a deep, calming breath and placing his hands on her shoulders "—listen to me, darling. There is nothing, I repeat, *nothing* wrong with my heart. Understand?"

His grim anger and the pinched look to his mouth didn't exactly reassure her. "It stopped during the surgery," she recited shakily. "And then while you were still in recovery, they had to...." She couldn't finish.

"Stop it!" Neil's fingers dug into her flesh until she winced. "It was shock, Lacey, and nothing more than that—shock due to loss of blood. The odds of it ever happening again are a million to one. I don't want you working yourself up over a problem that doesn't even exist, do you hear!"

She shook her head, unconvinced. "You can't know that for sure. If it happened once, it could happen again. And Bob also said you're supposed to be building up your strength again gradually. *Grad-*

ually, he said!" She was nearly hysterical now, her voice rising in distress. "And knowing that, you've been out here knocking down walls and painting ceilings—risking your life just to redecorate some rundown old house! It's stupid! *Stupid!*"

A muscle in Neil's jaw quivered as he visibly tried to control his temper. "It's not just a house," he said in hard, clipped syllables. "It's our *home*, or it will be, if you'll just stop being pigheaded long enough to be reasonable and *listen* to what I'm telling you!" His voice rose to a shout on the last six words as he gave her another hard shake.

"Don't!" she pleaded fearfully. "You mustn't upset yourself, Neil. Your blood pressure—"

He made a sound as if he was ready to explode, and Lacey's fingers twisted together nervously in front of her.

"I'll kill him," he vowed between clenched teeth. "So help me, I'll strangle him with my bare hands! *Lacey!* There is nothing *wrong* with my blasted blood pressure!"

Which was such a blatant untruth as he stood there red-faced, glowering at her, that Lacey could do nothing but shake her head sorrowfully and wring her hands.

Neil expelled a gusty breath and raked both hands through his hair as if he'd like to tear it out. "I honestly don't know whether to choke you or drag you outside into the trees and throw myself on you," he muttered in exasperation. "If it's not one thing, it's something else. You finally get over being afraid *of* me, and now you're afraid *for* me. Sweetheart, what can I do to convince you that I'm all right, that there's no cause for worry?"

Lacey was only partially listening to his earnest appeal. Her mind had snagged on a memory, an incident that had seemed odd at the time but now became clear.

"That day you came to the house, when you met the boys for the first time," she recalled with a frown. "You took something out of your pocket. It was some kind of medicine, wasn't it? Digitalis or something?"

"Or something," Neil admitted reluctantly. "They sent a prescription home with me, just in case I had any more episodes of tachycardia. The cardiologist told me that if it was going to happen at all, it would most likely be in the first couple of months, but that just in case I should carry medication for a year. Until that day, I swear, Lacey, I'd never needed to take it." His mouth quirked ironically as he went on.

"Actually, I doubt if I *needed* to then. It was just the shock of seeing the boys like that, with no warning. My heart was pounding a mile a minute, and I figured if anything would jolt it enough to stop it again, that was sure as hell the right time and place. So I panicked a little and took a pill," he added with a shrug. "*One* pill, in eight months!"

He moved toward her, a determined glint in his eye, and Lacey backed away from him nervously.

"No, Neil," she said with an emphatic shake of her head.

"No?" he repeated, grinning lazily. "I haven't even asked...yet."

"Don't think you can get around me with that sexy look and let's-go-to-bed voice," she told him firmly. "I'm not a fool. I know how much strain sex puts on the heart, and I won't have it on my conscience that I brought on another attack."

Neil drew a long, hissing breath. "Are you *trying* to provoke me, Lacey, because if you are, you're sure going about it the right way. Don't you ever refer to making love with me as 'sex' in that prissy tone of voice again!"

"I wasn't being prissy!" Lacey denied, gasping.

Neil pressed on. "That's the second or third time you've implied our lovemaking never meant more to you than a few minutes of physical pleasure."

"I never said that!" Lacey cried, and his eyes narrowed as he took a step closer.

"So you admit it was beautiful, almost mystical, then," he suggested silkily, his voice dropping half an octave as he continued to advance on her.

Lacey dodged away like a startled fawn. His words had conjured up unwelcome thoughts and memories, and the tip of her tongue came out to nervously moisten her lips.

"I didn't say that, either," she said evasively, and then she sucked in a sharp breath as she realized what he was doing. "Stop it! Just stop it, Neil. It won't work," she told him. She turned toward the door. "I'm going to check on the boys, and then I'm gong to get into my car and go home."

She half expected him to come after her or at least demand that she come back and stop running from him like a little coward—because she knew that was exactly what she was—but he only called out in a voice ringing with confidence, "This isn't finished, Lacey. Count on it—it's not finished by a long shot!"

She kept marching outside with long, determined strides, but her heart was filled with apprehension. When he used that tone of voice, she knew he meant business.

Mrs. Moore was due back on Sunday, which meant Lacey had to endure two more days of having Neil arrive at her house early and stay late. *He might as well move in bag and baggage*, she thought resentfully as she backed out of the drive Friday morning; he already acted like the master of the house. When he'd arrived with the boys this morning, he even had a bag of laundry, which he calmly informed her he intended to wash in her machine. Now *that* she'd like to be around to see, Lacey thought with amusement.

By the time she returned at five that afternoon the amusement had developed into a smug expectancy, which rapidly changed to stupefied astonishment when she looked out the window above the kitchen sink and saw Neil removing and folding sheets from her clothesline, assisted by their sons. As the bed linen came down, the row of laundry behind it became visible. A large lump formed in Lacey's throat at the sight of snowy white undershirts lined up side by side—the boys' looking like doll clothes next to Neil's.

He was relaxed and pleasant during dinner, but his eyes held an unmistakable message as they met hers frequently across the table, and Lacey braced herself for the battle she knew would begin as soon as the twins were tucked in for the night.

She tried to outmaneuver him by pointedly saying she thought she'd go to bed early, and she immediately regretted her choice of words when Neil smiled slowly and replied, "Sounds good to me," as he drew her into his arms. She knew good and well she only managed to wriggle free because he was still leery of using even the slightest degree of force to overcome her objections.

"Go home!" she told him rudely from the other side of the family room.

His wistful smile tugged at her heart, but she stiffened her back in determination and held out against it.

"It won't be 'home' until you and the boys are in it," he answered softly. "Home is where the heart is they say, so I guess right now *this* is my home."

"Never!" Lacey shot back, and his smile widened into a grin.

"You're really gorgeous, did you know that?" he said softly. "And I don't believe I've told you yet today how much I love you. Have I?"

Lacey gritted her teeth, drew a deep breath and counted to ten. "Will you *please* get out of my house?"

She heard the lack of conviction, the almost plaintive note in her voice, and her heart sank. He'd have heard it, too—he didn't miss a thing—and would take it for the weakening it was. She tensed for a move she knew he was about to make, but Neil suddenly seemed to switch tactics, throwing her off guard.

"I hear there's a dinner-dance out at the club tomorrow night. Come with me," he invited casually.

Lacey's brain scrabbled frantically to change direction and keep up with him, sensing a threat, but unsure of its source. "I . . . I can't," she stammered.

"Why not? Surely you can find somebody to watch the boys for a few hours on a Saturday night?"

"It's not that." She bit down hard on her lower lip, then confessed in a rush, "I've already promised to go with Paul."

Neil's eyes narrowed with menace, his lean body tensing. "You're pushing your luck, Lacey," he warned quietly.

"He asked me over a month ago," she said in her own defense. "You weren't even here then!"

"I'm here *now*. Just remember that, Lacey. I'm here now, for good." That it was a warning she didn't doubt. "I told you once that you couldn't hide behind other men, and I meant it," he added softly. And then, almost before she realized what was happening, he had turned on his heel and left the room. A minute later the sound of his truck's engine disturbed the silence of the quiet street as he left. Lacey didn't move for several minutes, and then she slowly turned out the lights and went to bed, to lie sleepless and tense for several hours.

ON SATURDAY NEIL behaved like a polite but reserved stranger, throwing her into an even deeper confusion. What's more, he didn't hang around after she returned home from work but left right away with the cool and obviously insincere statement that he hoped she enjoyed her night out.

Lacey glanced at her reflection once, not really seeing it, then picked up her bronze satin evening bag on its slender shoulder chain and left her bedroom. Sharon Crawford had willingly agreed to watch the boys, and they'd walked up the block half an hour ago, the pockets of their shorts stuffed full of *Star Wars* figures and Matchbox cars and trucks. A quick look at her watch showed the time to be seven-thirty. Paul would be here any minute, she realized nervously.

For the tenth time since he called the office that afternoon to let her know when to expect him, she wondered if she should have taken the opportunity to cancel their date. And for the tenth time she obstinately decided she'd been right not to. All right, so she was legally married to Neil; but they hadn't lived together as man and wife for eight years and didn't now. Why should she let his presence in the same town destroy her social life? She had a perfect right to go out with Paul or any other man, she told herself firmly, and ignored the nagging voice that disagreed.

Paul's look when she opened the door was comment enough on her appearance. She'd chosen a strapless red knee-length dress that was deceptively simple and intriguingly provocative at the same time. In addition to baring her upper chest and shoulders, the dress had one side slit to the thigh, and its material was a slinky silk blend that rippled over her curves like wet crimson paint. She seldom got the chance to wear something like this, and she knew she looked good in it even before she saw Paul's eyes light up with appreciation.

The club's dining room was already filling up when they arrived, and they were led to a table for eight in one corner. These dinner-dances were informally arranged mix-and-mingle affairs, and the only prerequisite was to phone in a reservation far enough in advance. There was one couple already seated at their table: Phil and Sherry Engel. The two couples knew each other well. They immediately fell into pleasant, relaxed conversation, and the evening seemed off to a good start.

It wasn't until about twenty minutes later, when Lacey had worked her way through half a Tom Collins, that Gary Baker arrived, looking distinctly upset as he held a chair for his wife, Emily. He didn't quite meet Lacey's eyes as he said a subdued hello and nervously remarked that he hadn't known she and Paul would be sharing their table, too.

"Where's Andy?" Sherry asked, and Lacey could have sworn Gary actually jumped in his seat, as if the question had startled him.

"Oh! She'll be along any time now, I expect," he replied, as his eyes darted toward the door. "Her, uh, her escort was picking her up."

Lacey and Paul exchanged puzzled frowns. Andrea was the Bakers' twenty-year-old daughter and a real knockout: blonde, blue-eyed and daintily petite. She was the apple of her parents' eyes, and normally they couldn't wait to show off her latest conquest. But

tonight Gary was behaving as though he almost
dreaded her arrival. His eyes kept sliding toward the
dining-room entrance as if he expected Attila the
Hun and a horde of invaders to come storming
through it any minute. Suddenly he sat bolt upright
in his chair and took a hasty gulp of his Bloody
Mary. When Lacey turned her head to see what had
caused such a reaction, she felt her stomach drop to
her knees.

How *dared* he! she thought furiously.

Neil stood at Andy's side, tall and infuriatingly at
ease as his eyes scanned the room until they came to
rest on the group at the corner table. And then a
satisfied smile touched his mouth, and he started
guiding Andy forward with a hand at her elbow.

The evening was ruined as far as Lacey was concerned, and she blamed Neil entirely. Phil happened
to serve on the club's membership committee, so
naturally he knew the situation; and it was obvious
from Sherry's and Em's embarrassed, stammered
greetings that their husbands had filled them in on
her relationship with Neil, too. To make matters
worse, Neil took the seat beside her, sandwiching her
between himself and Paul.

Dinner was an absolute debacle, and as soon as it
was finished both the Engels and the Bakers escaped
to the dance floor with a speed Lacey would have
found hilarious if she hadn't been so angry. Paul deftly and tactfully drew Andy along behind them, leaving Lacey and Neil alone.

"Just what do you think you're doing?" she demanded in a furious undertone. "You're old enough

to be her father, for heaven's sake! Don't you care what people are thinking?"

Neil casually draped an arm along the back of her chair, the sleeve of his jacket brushing her bare shoulders. He was so close she could smell his spicy aftershave and the odor of bourbon on his warm breath. He smiled into her eyes as his fingers idly stroked her arm.

"I never have, so why should I start now?" he drawled. "And technically, I'm old enough to be your father, too."

"Don't be ridiculous!" Lacey hissed. "You were never a father figure to me, and you know it."

When Neil's eyes narrowed with a sensual gleam she realized that she should have phrased that remark differently, and she averted her head in irritation. The next instant his head was bent close to her ear.

"I have to admit I never thought of you as a daughter, either," he told her in a deep-throated murmur that raised goose bumps on her nape. "From the second I set eyes on you, I only saw you in one role." His voice softened to a whisper as he added, "As my lover."

Lacey's breath stuck in her throat and her heart lurched in reaction.

"In my bed," he went on huskily. "Under me."

Her eyelids fluttered and her lips parted involuntarily, her breath finally shuddering free with a little gasping sound. "Stop!" she begged weakly, her eyes darting toward the couples at the next table.

Neil blithely ignored both the plea and her obvious distress. "Naked. Warm and eager. Soft everywhere

I'm hard. With your arms and legs wrapped around me, tight, like you never want to let go."

"Oh, Neil!" It came out a soft, quavering little moan. Lacey reached for the watered-down remains of her drink, but Neil's hand captured hers, his fingers curling around it warmly.

"You don't need that, baby," he breathed in her ear. "I can make you dizzy, if that's what you want. Come on." And then he was pulling her to her feet and onto the dance floor.

Lacey thought with a touch of hysteria that if he made her any dizzier she'd be staggering around the floor like a drunk. Neil directed her arms around his waist under his open jacket, so that she could feel his body heat and the solid firmness of his torso through the silk shirt he wore. He let his body take up the seduction his words had started as they swayed to the slow, romantic rhythm of the music. He held her pressed shamelessly close against him, his thighs rubbing hers while his hips tormented with gentle back-and-forth movements that sent pulsing jolts of desire racing through her bloodstream. She suddenly became aware that he was steering them toward the sliding glass doors at the end of the room, where the building opened onto the pool deck.

"No," she tried to protest, but she couldn't seem to inject any authority into her breathlessly weak voice.

And then they were outside in the sultry summer night. Lacey tried once more to stop him as he pulled her around the corner, both arms still securely around her.

"The lights aren't on." *What an asinine, idiotic*

thing to say, she thought as she felt the rough pressure of bricks against her back, still warm from the sun's heat.

"I've loved you in the dark before," Neil murmured in a soft growl as he held her in place with his body. "Remember?"

He didn't give her a chance to answer, his arms cushioning her as he drove her back against the wall, making her aware of every inch of his body with every inch of hers. His mouth was open and hungry, not allowing even a second for thought or hesitation as it devoured hers.

"Remember, Lacey?" he repeated as he dragged his lips to her ear. "Remember what we used to do to each other with our mouths? You know how to drive me absolutely wild. I want you to do all that again, and I'll. . . ." The rest was breathed hotly into her ear, punctuated by the darting flick of his tongue.

Lacey moved her head from side to side, trying desperately not to listen to his erotic promises, frantic to resist the effect he was having on her love-starved senses.

"No," she gasped. "No, Neil! Your heart!"

He placed one of her hands over it. "Does that feel like a weak heart to you darling? Admit it—it's about to come right through my rib cage!" Then, with a note of irony underlying the passion in his voice, he added: "You think making love would put a strain on it. . . . Let me tell you, Lacey, it couldn't be any worse than the frustration I've lived with for the past month, every time I get close to you."

She looked up at him, the doubt and fear in her

eyes slowly clearing as they met the unbridled passion in his. Beneath her hand his heart hammered out a strong, regular tattoo that exactly matched hers.

"Where are the boys?" he asked softly as he bent to kiss her lips.

"At the Crawfords'. Until midnight," Lacey answered just as softly against his mouth as her hands crept up to bury themselves in his luxuriant hair.

He glanced at his watch. "It's almost nine. That gives us three uninterrupted hours. I wonder how many times, in how many ways, I can satisfy you in three hours."

Lacey's eyes closed, and her head sagged back against the bricks. If not for the fact that he had her pinned to the wall with his body, she knew she'd have slithered bonelessly down to the cement pool deck.

"Andy," she whispered, her voice weak and tremulous. "You can't just go off and leave her here."

She felt Neil's lips curve into a smile as his mouth caressed the side of her neck. "She really wants to be with your buddy Paulo. I notice you don't seem too concerned about leaving *him* in the lurch," he pointed out, to Lacey's embarrassment. "She's nuts about him, but he thinks he's too old for her. She figured if he saw her out with a senile old coot like me, he might change his mind. I doubt if either of them would complain if we switched partners for the rest of the night." He kissed her hard, his hand fondling her breast with a gentle urgency. "Now come on, our time's running out."

Paul and Andy were the only two at the table

when they returned to the dining room. Neil informed them calmly that he was taking his wife home now, then handed Lacey her bag and wrapped a possessive arm around her waist to guide her to the door. She marveled at his smooth self-assurance when she felt the dozen or so pairs of eyes on them as they left.

When they pulled into her driveway Neil turned to her, his hand coming up to softly stroke the curve of her jaw.

"Worried?" he asked quietly.

Lacey nodded. "I can't help it. My mind's just too busy," she said with a nervous catch in her voice.

He slid across the bench seat to take her in his arms, tilting her head back. "Then I guess I'll just have to provide a focus for your thoughts, won't I?"

10

HE TOOK HER KEY and let them into the house, turning on only the entry light to guide the way upstairs. In her bedroom, too, he switched on a single lamp on her dresser. It was as if he knew she needed darkness, or at least the shadows of half light.

The intense level of sexual expectancy had diminished somewhat in the time it took to drive from the club; but now, in the empty, silent house, it built swiftly again until the air seemed to throb with a pulse of its own. Lacey removed the gold earrings, which were the only jewelry she wore, and her fingers felt stiff and clumsy. Behind her Neil moved almost silently, only the faint rustle of cloth betraying his presence in the room. Finally he came up behind her as she stood facing the dresser mirror. He'd removed his jacket, and the muted glow of the lamp made his silk shirt look almost iridescent as the light was absorbed in one spot and refracted in another. It gave him a magical quality as he moved, as if he weren't quite real, not a flesh-and-blood man but some spectral visitor who might vanish if she attempted to touch him.

And then his hands lifted to her shoulders, and the illusion was destroyed.

Slowly, oh, so slowly, his hard, warm palms glided up her shoulders to curve around her neck, his thumbs raising goose flesh at her nape as they stroked with a feather-light touch. In the mirror his eyes met and held hers, and his soft, tender smile caught Lacey's breath. She could hear the furious pounding of her heart and feel the sudden clenching of the muscles in her throat. Lacey recognized the symptoms for what they were: basic gut-level desire. She wanted him so badly that she literally ached for him. Oh, it had been so long. So long. And she needed him so desperately, with her hands and mouth and every square inch of her. Did he know? Could he feel the storm raging inside her, through her flesh?

"You're tense." Neil's fingers began to gently massage her neck and shoulders. "Is it just nerves, or something else?"

Lacey tried to answer, couldn't, cleared her throat and tried again. "Something else." Was that her voice—that rusty, hoarse rasp?

Only when Neil sighed and she felt his hands relax did she realize how tense *he* had been. Ridiculously, it helped. She felt her body let go; a long, pent-up breath escaped her as her head fell back against his chest, her eyes closing. Neil's lips touched her skin, burning, tormenting.

"You're so brown," he murmured. "Have you been sunbathing in the nude?"

"No. My bathing suit has a strap that comes off, so it won't leave any white marks."

Inconsequential talk, meaningless words to keep them both from dwelling too long on what was about to happen. *Why?* Lacey wondered in bemusement. This was what they both wanted, wasn't it? What they both *craved*. Then she knew. He was deliberately trying to put her at ease, still believing she was nervous, or afraid, or both. And maybe—just maybe—he was a little nervous, too. Once she got over her initial surprise at the thought, she found it not all that hard to accept. The last of her outer tension dissolved, leaving only the coiled passion inside, waiting to be released.

Neil's hands suddenly moved, dropping to the elasticized top of her dress. Without speaking he pushed it down all the way to her waist. Lacey stood quietly as his hands slid over the rounded smoothness of her breasts and then clasped them gently from underneath, pressing upward so that the erect nipples were clearly visible in the mirror.

Without looking, she knew that his eyes were fixed on her reflection, and she was glad that her body was still firm and fit. *Let him look*, she thought proudly; *let him see his fill and know that it's all his—that no other man has ever viewed or touched or possessed what has always been his alone.*

She rolled her head on his chest, her eyes still closed and a dreamy smile on her lips as her cheek brushed his bent head. She breathed his name, softly, making it sound almost like a prayer.

"So perfect," Neil whispered. His hands suddenly trembled, and she knew that despite his restraint he was every bit as hungry for her as she was for him. Yet still he held back, displaying a patience she wouldn't have believed him capable of as he let his hands and softly roving lips bring her to an even more intense awareness of him, until every nerve screamed for more—*more*!

He must have known, because his hands reluctantly left her breasts to push the dress off her body, and with it, the half-slip she wore under it. Lacey was thankful for its elastic, as the waist and bodice slid easily over her hips. A second later the garments whispered to her feet, and she stepped free of them without so much as losing contact with Neil's hard chest.

His arms came around her to steady her as she removed her shoes, rubbing against him in the process a little more than was absolutely necessary. When she heard his sharply indrawn breath, a thrill shot through her all the way to her toes. And then her own breath caught as his hands moved, shifted, to clasp her lower, the heel of his palm hard against her as his fingers burned through the thin silk of her bikini panties. He knew exactly where to press, where to stroke—no fumbling or groping here, no indeed. But what was he trying to do, drive her completely insane?

"Want me, Lacey."

His voice was a harsh rasp in her ear as he forced her back against him and thrust his hips gently, his busy fingers increasing the torment as they sent white-hot needles of desire shooting upward and outward.

"Want me so much you can't think of anything else, not the past or the future, nothing but here and now, and what I can give you."

She groaned—not a soft, weak, ladylike moan of submission, but a deep, hungry sound like a predatory female animal. And then she was turning, twisting around in his arms and pushing herself against him as her hands reached out, fingers curled like talons to grasp at him, clutching with mindless urgency as she found his mouth and ground hers against it.

She felt his startled gasp, the momentary shocked tensing of his body, and then it was as if she'd set a match to tinder. His arms squeezed her mercilessly as he strained toward her, chest and belly, hips and thighs pressing, seeking contact with her softness through the flimsy barrier of his clothes. He was trembling she realized joyfully; not just his hands anymore, but all of him, shaking uncontrollably.

And then suddenly he wrenched his head away, drawing a deep, painful breath as he clenched his jaw and pressed her head down onto his chest.

"Lacey," he gasped. "I can't.... This isn't the way I planned it. You—" He swallowed hard, as if something big and dry had stuck in his throat. "It's happening too fast. Slow down. Slow down, baby, and let me—"

"No," she moaned, and pushed against him, hard, making him shudder and groan helplessly. "I don't want to slow down. Now, Neil. Take me now. I want you inside me.... Oh, hurry, please."

"Lacey," he whispered in a shaken voice as another massive tremor shook him. But then he forced her to ease away a little, lifting her face to him as he gazed down at her with those amazing copper eyes.

"You *wonder*!" he breathed, and his voice held joy and triumph as well as passion. "You beautiful, impossibly perfect wonder! You really mean it, don't you? *Lacey!*"

He kept repeating her name, over and over between hard, fervent kisses while she clutched at his shoulders to keep herself upright. And then he suddenly switched tactics again, his hands stroking and soothing, gentling her until at last she managed to gain some control over her desire. It was still there; she wanted him as much as—if not more than—she ever had in her life, but now she had the panting creature inside her on a leash. She stared up at him, waiting, knowing he wasn't going to take her until he was good and ready; and the waiting—the expectancy—served to inflame them both even more.

"Undress me," Neil whispered in a voice he was helpless to keep from catching.

Lacey saw the immensity of his need, the torment he was enduring to restrain it, and a smile tilted the corners of her mouth as she let her hands slide down the front of his shirt until they reached the snug waist of his trousers. Slowly, an inch at a time, she pulled the shirt free, her knuckles pressing against him only to withdraw again, prolonging his agony.

"You're so gorgeous in these clothes, it's almost a shame to take them off," she murmured. "Tell me," as her fingers worked at his buttons with excruciating slowness, "did you wear a silk shirt on purpose tonight with me in mind?"

She was remembering how he'd taught her about silk; how erotic it was against the skin; that when the fingers moved over it, the tactile sense perceived everything it covered with heightened awareness.

"Could be," Neil answered huskily. "Did you wear that sexy red thing with *me* in mind?"

Her chuckle was deep and throaty as she shook her head. "I didn't even know you'd be there."

"Are you sure about that?" Neil challenged. "You know me better than to think I'd sit by and let some other man trespass on my property. I think you had me in the back of your mind when you picked that dress, because you knew tonight would have to end with me taking it off."

Had she? Lacey didn't know. What's more, she didn't care. "Maybe so," she whispered as his shirt fell to the floor, and she wrestled with the hook fastening of his pants. "All I know for sure is what's on my mind right now. Neil, don't just stand there! This stupid thing won't—"

His hands moved, and the next thing she knew he had her clasped high in his arms and was crossing the floor to her bed. The spread and sheet were already turned back, ready to receive them as he placed her squarely in the center of the mattress and then joined her. Her panties and his socks went flying in three different directions, and then he was propped above her, grinning down at her like a hungry wolf.

"Now," he murmured seductively, "just what was it you had on your mind, Mrs. Hartmann?"

She groaned as she reached for his head to pull him down, and his grin abruptly disappeared.

He paused just before he finally—*finally*—moved over her to mutter hoarsely, "Are you afraid?"

"Yes," Lacey managed. "I'm afraid I'll lose my mind if you don't stop torturing me. Oh, God, Neil! Please—"

His mouth muffled the rest of the plea as one knee nudged at her thighs, and they parted eagerly. Again he hesitated, his chest heaving with his labored breathing.

"Lacey, it's been eight years."

"I know. I *know!* Oh, Neil, don't you know what you're doing to me!"

"Darling, listen!" he said urgently. "I'm trying to tell you—" His voice suddenly strained, he caught her head in his hands and stared hard into her eyes. "I'll probably hurt you. I'll try not to, but I don't think—"

"I don't care! I don't *care!*" Her head twisted on the pillow, her hands clutching at him in an impatient frenzy. She was half mad with frustration, her body poised and ready while he continued to deny it. "Just please, *please* don't make me wait anymore!"

Neil went absolutely still, the breath held in his throat for what seemed an eternity before it rushed from him on a sighing moan. His eyes flared with a wild surge of elation, and then, before Lacey could tense in preparation, he joined their bodies with one decisive thrust.

Neither moved for timeless seconds, each savoring the wonder and the joy of once more being united, no longer an incomplete half but a single, perfectly formed whole. Neil spoke his thoughts aloud, his voice rough and unsteady.

"It's like coming home."

"Yes," Lacey whispered. "Welcome back, darling. I didn't know how much I'd missed you."

"Oh, Lacey!" Though his voice was muffled by her skin, she could still hear the emotion choking it. He lifted his head slightly, his eyes dark and searching. "Are you all right?"

"Better," she said with a soft smile, "but still not quite all right. Love me, Neil," she urged. "Please, love me."

"I do," he answered hoarsely as he began to move. "Oh, Lacey, I do! You'll never know how much."

It was beautiful, perfect, a flight beyond the moon and stars to another place, where nothing existed but the pleasure each gave and received, until at last they collapsed, spent and breathless and still locked together, loath to move apart, limbs entwined and flesh pressed eagerly to flesh. Tears ran unchecked down Lacey's face, and Neil kissed them away with tender concern.

"Darling, what is it?" he asked when her storm of weeping showed no sign of abating.

The anxiety in his eyes was more than she could bear, because she knew the reason for it. She cried out a soft protest as she reached for his mouth, pressing salty kisses on his lips while her trembling hands stroked the lean planes of his face.

"No," she wept in remorse. "No, don't look at me like that. I—" She drew a ragged breath and then confessed the reason for her tears. "I love you. Oh, Neil, I love you so much!"

The muscles in his arms quivered as he drew her

closer, gathering her in as if she was a small child who needed comforting.

"Well, for heaven's sake, is that anything to cry about?" he teased, but his voice was suspiciously shaky. Then his hold suddenly tightened, and he buried his face in her neck. "I was afraid that I'd never hear you say it again," he muttered fiercely.

"Oh, Neil, I'm sorry. So sorry," Lacey sobbed. "To think of what we've missed, what *you've* missed— the boys, watching them grow, being with them. I've cheated both you and them, not to mention myself. How you must hate me!"

"Hate you?" he repeated with a shaky laugh. "How could I hate you, you impossible woman, when I love you more than life itself? If anybody has a right to hate, it's you, after what I—"

"No." Lacey stopped him with her mouth. "No," she said again, her voice strong and sure as she wrapped her arms more securely around him and burrowed into his chest. Her tears had stopped, and the smile she gave him was sublimely happy.

"You can really forgive me?" Neil asked, his eyes intent as they probed hers.

"If you need my forgiveness, yes," she answered softly. "As long as you forgive me for all those wasted years."

Neil shook his head, unsmiling. "They don't matter. Nothing matters anymore except that we're together now—all four of us. I couldn't stand to lose you again, not now, not after tonight."

His deep voice shook with intensity, and Lacey

was moved to tears again by the awesome yearning in his eyes.

"No," she agreed huskily. "Not after tonight. I couldn't stand to lose you, either." Then she smiled slowly as her legs twined around his in a silken caress. "Now. At least an hour of our three must be gone already, Mr. Hartmann, and I seem to recall you made some kind of challenge—or was it a threat—about how many times you could. . . ."

She never finished the sentence as he proceeded to follow through on the promise, for that was what it turned out to be. Later, he left the bed. She murmured a questioning protest, and he leaned over her to whisper that he was going to collect their sons and for her to keep his place for him. When he returned, she was asleep. He woke her with teasing kisses, and Lacey turned into his arms happily. She fell asleep again still locked in their firm embrace.

LATER SHE LAY curled against Neil's side, one slender leg flung over his and her head resting contentedly on his chest.

"You want to get under the covers?" he asked humorously as he ran a lazy hand down her side to the curve of her hip.

"No, I don't want to move. Not yet." Her fingers glided over his stomach in a teasing caress, and she turned her head an inch to press her lips to his warm skin. "I love you, Mr. Hartmann," she murmured.

Neil shifted her closer, resting his cheek against her hair. "And I love you, Mrs. Hartmann. You and those two sons of ours. I still have trouble believing you're all really mine."

Hearing the vibrant note in his deep voice, Lacey wondered how she could ever have questioned his love. She smiled softly against his chest.

"I've been thinking...since you're such an outstanding success in the daddy department, how would you feel about trying for another set of twins?"

Neil raised his head in surprise, and she lifted hers to smile at him.

"You're kidding, aren't you?" He sounded uncertain.

"I've never been more serious in my life. Well? What do you think?"

He laughed in disbelief. "Lacey, I'm forty-five years old! I'd be...I'd be sixty-four by the time she's ready for college!"

"So? You'll be a very young six— *She?* Did you say *she?*"

"Well, if we're going to do it, I'd really like a girl this time," he said in a perfectly serious tone.

And then Lacey was suddenly on her back, and he was propped over her on an elbow, grinning down at her.

"Oh, Neil!" She smiled ecstatically, reaching up to smooth her palms over his hair. "A little sister for the boys. They'd be thrilled."

"No more than their old man," he murmured. And then a wicked light came into his eyes. "Besides, another baby would be a surefire way to keep you at home."

Lacey smiled, outwardly submissive but knowing that she could never be content as a full-time hausfrau. "I could always take her along to the office," she suggested tentatively. "That's what I did with the boys."

The light in Neil's eyes faded, and he gazed at her solemnly. "But that wouldn't be necessary this time," he pointed out. "Lacey, for heaven's sake, you've got a rich husband who's just dying to spoil you rotten. You've proved yourself, darling. Can't you let me take care of you now, provide for you? I'm not asking so much, am I?"

From his point of view, she supposed not. And she didn't want this single bone of contention to spoil the happiness they'd finally found.

"Try to understand," she asked, her voice soft and sincere. "What you're asking is that I give up my identity, that I stop being *me*, Lacey Hartmann, and become Neil's wife or Todd and Scott's mommy. It's taken me eight long years to become a person in my own right, Neil, a person I can like and respect. Don't ask me to give up what I've worked so hard to gain."

His jaw set obstinately. "*I* gave up a multimillion-dollar business," he reminded her.

"That's not fair! In the first place, it's not the same for a man, and you know it. *You* don't have to prove you're capable of supporting yourselves and your families! And in the second place, you'd already decided to sell out before you even came here, so don't try to pretend you made some big sacrifice for my sake!"

He rolled to his back with a frown of irritation—or was it disgust?

"You even argue like a man," he muttered, scowling up at the ceiling. "The thing is," he admitted with reluctance, "I just don't like sharing you with other people, especially not strangers I don't even know."

An amused smile tugged at Lacey's mouth as she snuggled up at his side. "Now you know how millions of women all over the world have felt for years," she told him indulgently. Then a thought occurred to her, and she looked at him closely. "Does it bother you...threaten you, to be the one who's keeping the home fires burning?"

"Are you kidding?" he murmured. "I'm having the time of my life. I've had my fill of the rat race. I just wish you could say the same."

"Maybe I will, when I've been at it as long as you."

"I'll be ready for the old folks' home by then!" His head turned and he looked into her eyes, his expression somber. "You're just not going to give in, are you?"

Lacey shook her head. "I'm sorry, Neil, I can't."

He pulled her on top of him, his hands warm on her skin. "Then it looks like we're going to have to compromise. How's this—you agree to stay home for a while after the baby comes, let Rick run the business. I doubt if he'll drive you into bankruptcy in a few short weeks."

"I think I could live with that," Lacey agreed willingly. "And what will your part of this compromise be?"

He grinned wryly. "Oh, learning to change diapers and heat up bottles of formula and keeping dinner warm when you're late getting home, and.... Dear Lord, I can see a life of drudgery stretching ahead of me already."

Lacey reached up to bury her fingers in his thick hair. "Will you really mind all that much?"

His rich laugh took her by surprise just before he deftly flipped her onto her back. "Mind? You little idiot, it sounds like heaven, compared to what I've been used to all my life."

He kissed her hard, then smiled down at her lovingly.

"You fraud!" Lacey accused as she smiled back. "You were ready to see things my way all along, weren't you?"

"I wanted to find out just how sure you are of what you want, and how willing you are to fight for it. Lacey, I'm so damned proud of you! You're strong and resilient and not afraid to stand your ground when you know you're right. I wouldn't trade you for that timid child you were eight years ago, not for anything. I can't even regret those lost years, because if we'd stayed together you'd never have grown into the woman you are today."

His voice was soft and deep, filled with the same emotion shining in his incredible eyes. Tears of happiness glistened on Lacey's lashes as her fingers stroked his hard face.

"I love you, Neil," she murmured, her voice moist and a little thick.

He lowered his head to whisper huskily, "Prove it."

And, as their bodies melted together, Lacey finally felt the past ebb away. Together they would build a *new* life, create *new* memories to share. Her lips curved in a joyful smile as she vowed that this one would be the first of many, many more.

THE AUTHOR

Lynn Turner's love of books has played an important part in her life. She spends her mornings teaching remedial reading to children; her afternoons are devoted to writing fiction.

Lynn says that the theme of *For Now, For Always* is "never to give up hope."